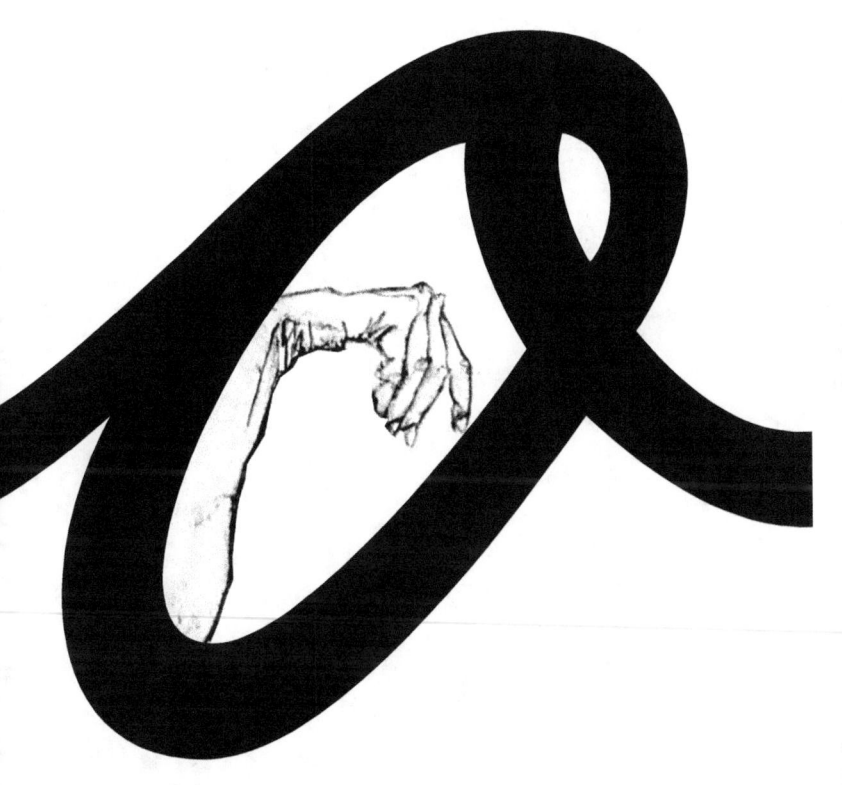

Ferit Edgü

Noone

TRANSLATED *by*

FULYA PEKER

Contra Mundum Press   New York · London · Melbourne

Translation of *Kimse* © 2015 Fulya Peker. Originally published in the Turkish language under the title *Kimse* © 1988, Ferit Edgü; © 2013 Sel Yayıncılık. Published by arrangement via Anatolia Lit Agency.

First Contra Mundum Press Edition 2015.

Library of Congress Cataloguing-in-Publication Data

Edgü, Ferit, 1936–

[Kimse. English.]

Noone / Fulya Peker; translated from the original Turkish by Fulya Peker

—1st Contra Mundum Press Edition

186 pp., 5×8 in.

ISBN 9781940625157

I. Edgü, Ferit
II. Title.
III. Peker, Fulya.
IV. Translator.
V. Preface.

2015953090

This publication was aided by a subvention from the Türkiye Cumhuriyeti Kültür ve Turizm Bakanlığı [Republic of Turkey Ministry of Culture and Tourism]. The Universal Journey of Turkish Culture

Written between 1964 & 1974, between Paris & Hakkari, Ferit Edgü's Noone approaches politics from a poetic standpoint and transforms a social-realist setting into a metaphor for a self that is in search of a subject for a sentence, or rather, that is subjected to a sentence.

As a record of history that is both personal & universal, Edgü depicts in Noone the severity of alienation, the difficulty of communication, the importance of memory, and the hidden rhyme of 'existential' & 'survival,' two grand words often pronounced by pronouns suffering oppression & isolation. Noone compels us to consider the politically imposed idea of "the other" and how this "other" is not somewhere outside, external to us, but within. It prompts us to reflect on questions concerning the failure, or inability, to communicate, not only with others, but with one's self due to man-made borders, whether lingual or geopolitical. Edgü's acute & subtle observations about adverse living conditions that reduce humans to creatures of mere subsistence echo not only the current political climate in eastern Turkey, but also the general state in many parts of the world.

While people are constantly forced to be 'noone,' the traces of history are buried (or frozen) under snow, & memory is dismantled, Noone reminds us of tomorrow, by re-momenting the past & keeping a record of the moment.

Ferit Edgü

Noone

Noone

Selections from conversations had for a certain period
of time (through a severe winter) in a certain place
(on the east side of our country, a mountain village called
Pirkanis, with thirteen houses and a population
of 100 people), to recall, to remoment, to recognize,
to question, to look for a response, & especially
to survive; or an attempt (ation) to transform
a monologue into a dialogue.

Presentation

Haven't you ever, on a May night, hung your wish on a rose branch? says A Voice.

What wish? says the Other Voice. Which wish? Which rose branch? When? Why? How? Where?

Any one of your wishes, says That Voice. For example, a quiet home in a garden. For example, a motherly woman, who would warm your bed. For example, your own child, who would keep your name alive. For example, a change in your life.

On a rose branch? says the Other Voice.

Or a book, says the Firsttospeak Voice.

A holy book? the Other Voice answers (sarcastic) by asking.

Why not? says the Initial Voice.

But that was written long ago, says the Last Voice.

Maybe you would also want to write one, says the Stubborn Voice.

Others wrote what I wanted to write, says the Faithful Voice. And so long ago. And I'm not complaining about it.

Thus, my book is rolled up, you mean to say? says the Alwaysasking Voice.

No, screwed up, says the Loser Voice.

*Maybe for that reason you hung your wish on a rose branch, in a warm Hıdırellez night; maybe it swayed on the branch till the morning, when you went to look at it in the morning …
Work it out, try to remoment, says the Persistent Voice.*

Why did you bring this subject up? What do you want from me? says the Broken Voice.

Because if you are rain, I am earth, says the Ramshackled Voice.

I am an un-falling rain, at the most, says That Voice.

And I am a milk-less baby, crying & agonizing; an offering for the god that brings down the rain, says the Other Voice.

You are the moon, and I am the sun; you are the one that turns back on me, I am the one that burns for you; I will tell you about my grand love on the day of the apocalypse.

Tell me now, says Gettingaway Voice. Today is the day of the apocalypse.

No need to tell, says the Answering Voice. But if you wish we can talk.

What else do we do anyway? says the Still Voice.

Let's begin, says the Blowinginthewind Voice.

Part I

Ah on a mountaintop
to look for one's self
on a winter night
as the snow
covers all the traces

To say that I've not gone out, says the First Voice. Out, to the outhouse. For three days. Maybe four. Maybe even five. To say that I've not gone.

Why? says the Second Voice. You should've gone out & tried.

In such cold weather? answers the First Voice.

Your intestines've gotten dry. Go out & try. Stop being lazy, the Second Voice insists.

Let them get dry, says the First Voice. I don't intend to freeze.

Dogs are howling, don't you hear? It's snowing. It was flaky; now it's turned into a blizzard. Frost. To go out in this frost. Out, to the outhouse. Going there to try loosening these dried intestines. NO! NO! Moreover, the path to the outhouse might be covered with snow.

Then, try in front of the door, outside, says the Second Voice.

In front of the door? says the First Voice.

Sure, says the Second Voice. Why not? Snow would cover it and it would freeze. It wouldn't smell till summer. Of course if it's not eaten by the dogs right after you come back. (He laughs.)

I'm afraid of catching a cold, whines the First Voice.

Ah, I understand, says the Second Voice. Then try one of the corners of the room.

That's a good idea, says the First Voice. But there's nothing to try.

However you like, says the Second Voice. Then don't whine.

There is noone whining, says the First Voice.

They remain silent.

After a while, the First Voice begins to speak: "Whenever ..." but couldn't end his sentence.

The other curiously waits for the end of the sentence. The end of the sentence does not arrive.

The ones that arrive (from outside) are the north wind's whistle (vuuuuu) and the howl of dogs (huuu-uuuuu-uu-uu-uu) & (from inside) the crackle of dung in the stove.

Considering the howling dogs — begins the First Voice.

Yes, the Second Voice completes, the wolves must've come out.

They remain silent.

They listen to the howling dogs & the whistling north wind.

Then, the First Voice says, and you want me to go out & try.

You can try in front of the door, says the Second Voice.

You forgot what happened to me the last time, says the First Voice. Plus, there's nothing to try. I told you. I said that my intestines are dry.

Then an enema, suggests the Second Voice.

Are you kidding me? says the First Voice.

At least a piece of soap, says the Second Voice.

There you go, that's a good idea, says the First Voice. But not now. Tomorrow we can try that.

Tomorrow, after daybreak. After the wolves withdraw to the mountains. After the danger is over.

Why are you waiting for tomorrow, says the Second Voice.

As I've said, now the wolves, says the First Voice. Now the wolves & danger.

Right, says the Second Voice.

They remain silent for a while.

Then the Second Voice asks, Shall we light the lamp? What do you say?

No need, replies the First Voice.

But it's too dark, insists the Second Voice.

So what? rebuffs the First Voice. For whom will you light the lamp? To see whom?

For myself, says the wobbly Second Voice. To be in the light.

For yourself? asks the First Voice.

Yes, says the Second Voice.

Are you afraid? says the First Voice?

Yes, says the Second Voice.

Of whom are you afraid? says (sarcastically) the First Voice.

I don't know, says the Second Voice.

The door is bolted, you know, says the First Voice.

Yes, says the Second Voice.

The shutters are pulled down. No person can enter, says the First Voice.

And no animal, says the Second Voice.

If so? says the First Voice.

I don't know, says the Second Voice. I'm afraid. A moment. Then: You too are afraid.

The First Voice does not answer.

If you weren't afraid, you'd go out and try, says the Second Voice.

I told you that there's nothing to try, says the First Voice. My fear is of catching a cold. To get a cold, and to lay down and die on this mountaintop. My fear is to be devoured by dogs & wolves while trying to empty out my dry intestines.

To be what? asks the Second Voice.

To be devoured, repeats the First Voice.

So you don't want to light the lamp, says the Second Voice (who hasn't been listening to or hearing the answer).

I said there's no need, says the First Voice.

Then let's go to bed, says the Second Voice.

Good idea, says the First Voice.

Won't you undress? says the Second Voice.

No, says the First Voice.

They remain silent.

Then, the Second Voice says, Do you hear the dogs howling?

I hear, says the First Voice.

They aren't howling any longer. They stopped howling, do you hear? says the Second Voice.

I hear, says the First Voice.

They must be chasing the wolves, says the Second Voice.

Their bones will be found on the river tomorrow, says the First Voice.

Only if not covered by the snow, says the Second Voice.

If not covered, says the First Voice.

If so only by the summer, says the Second Voice.

Right, says the First Voice.

They remain silent.

Then, the First Voice asks, The batteries ran out, right?

Long agooo, says the Second Voice.

Shall we warm them up & try again, says the First Voice.

We tried many times, says the Second Voice.

Right, says the First Voice. Then: When would they come?

What? asks the Second Voice.

The batteries, says the First Voice.

God knows, says the Second Voice. If someone goes to town. If they've any left in town. If the road is not closed. Then: Why did you ask?

No reason, says the First Voice.

Are you bored? asks the Second Voice.

Not boredom, says the First Voice. I forgot to get bored long ago. This is, — for a voice.

What, for a voice? asks the Second Voice.

Need, says the First Voice.

Need for what voice? asks the Second Voice.

A human voice, says the First Voice.

This, I'm baffled, says the Second Voice.

What is there to be baffled about? says the First Voice.

Human … here … on this mountaintop, there are human … human voices, says the Second Voice.

I don't understand the language of these people, says the First Voice.

Whose language do you understand? says the Second Voice.

The First Voice doesn't answer this question.

From where did I come to here? says the First Voice.

From where did we come to here? the Second Voice echœs the question.

Instead of an answer, they ask one another the question: "From where did we come to here?", but just for the sake of it, quietly, maybe they don't even hear one another.

As if I ran away, ran away to this mountaintop here, couldn't find another place to go, as if to be forgotten, says the First Voice.

Something like that, says the Second Voice.

What else could we've done? says the First Voice.

We could've run away to somewhere else, says the Second Voice.

Somewhere warm. To an island or a desert, says the First Voice.

There are waves on islands, day and night, says the Second Voice. And sand storms in deserts.

We could've taken shelter in a forest, says the First Voice.

You've obviously never listened to the trees talking in the wind, says the Second Voice.

Then it's good here, says the First Voice. Is that what you mean?

I don't know if it's good or bad, says the Second Voice. We are here, that's all I know.

But we've to cast off from here, says the First Voice.

We will, says the Second Voice. We've cast off from many places. We'll cast off from here also. We'll run away. From this snowy mountaintop. Here is not for us. We'll go down to the lowlands. We'll roam around by the sea. On the sand that may burn our feet. All naked. Under the summer sun. In the south somewhere.

Then?

Then we'll run away from there also, for sure, says the First Voice.

To where? says the Second Voice.

How can I know it today? says the First Voice. But the day will come; we'll run away from there also.

But one day we'll stop. Somewhere, we'll cast anchor on still waters, won't we? says the Second Voice.

Yes, says the First Voice. One day. Somewhere. To dig our pit and get in.

Move a little further, says the Second Voice.

Be still. Let it be. Sit and stay where you sit, says the First Voice.

I'm not sitting, I'm lying down, says the Second Voice.

Lie down and stay where you lie — never to stand up, says the First Voice.

They remain silent.

Then (again) the Second Voice begins: Do you hear the rattling?

No, says the First Voice. I hear nothing.

Weird, I also don't hear it any longer, says the Second Voice.

So? says (angry) the First Voice.

But I felt like hearing, says the Second Voice.

Hearing what? says the First Voice.

The rattling, says the Second Voice.

Listen to yourself instead of the rattling, says the First Voice.

To do what? says the Second Voice.

Haven't you ever asked? says the First Voice.

Asked what? says the Second Voice.

Everything, says the First Voice.

For example? says the Second Voice.

For example, why're you here? says the First Voice.

Why am I here? asks the Second Voice. Then answers: Because you're here.

Right, says the First Voice. Then adds: What if we weren't here?

We'd be somewhere else, says the Second Voice.

Somewhere else? Where? says the First Voice.

I don't know, says the Second Voice. For example in Paris.

We were there, says the First Voice.

But we ran away, says the Second Voice.

If we weren't in Paris? says the First Voice.

In London, Rome, Madrid, Karachi, says the Second Voice.

Don't make me laugh, says the First Voice.

In Moscow, Florida, Addis Ababa, says the Second Voice.

Yes, says the First Voice. Why not?

They laugh. With laughter, holding their groins.

After their laughter subsides, the First Voice asks: Where would you want to be now?

Nowhere, says the Second Voice.

But you're here now, says the First Voice.

Yes, I'm here now, fortunately, says the First Voice. It could've been worse than the worst.

Worse than the worst? says the Second Voice. What do you mean?

You never know, says the First Voice. At least we're under a roof in here.

Right, says the Second Voice. Our room isn't as cold.

Not as cold? says the First Voice, with his teeth chattering.

Compared to outside, says the Second Voice.

Compared to outside, yes. But we could've been somewhere warmer. For example, at a public bath. On the navel stone. Our dirt coming off of our skin. Or in a warm hotel room, sweating, enfolded in the arms of a woman whose name we don't even know.

No doubt, says the Second Voice. We could've.

Then why're you always thinking of the worst? says the First Voice. Why always worse than the worst.

You know what, while sleeping a while ago, I was thinking in my dream, says the Second Voice.

You slept? says (befuddled) the First Voice.

Haven't you slept? says (befuddled) the Second Voice.

Not quite, says the First Voice.

In my dream I thought … the Second Voice tries to continue.

You're always like this, interrupts the First Voice. You think in your dream, and dream when awake.

I can't help it, answers the Second Voice.

Noone can help it, says (sighing) the First Voice. There's no reason to get embarrassed about it.

That's what I wanted to say, says the Second Voice.

They remain silent.

Then the First Voice says: What were you thinking of in your dream?

I forget, says the Second Voice.

Good, says the First Voice.

They remain silent.

Then, the First Voice says: Do you hear?

Hear what? asks the Second Voice.

The dogs, says the First Voice.

Yes, says the Second Voice.

They probably locked them in the sheepfold. Scared of the wolves.

The wolves got down, you say? says the First Voice.

They got down I say, says the Second Voice.

Shall we look out the window? says the First Voice.

They can be seen, you say? says the Second Voice.

I suppose, says the First Voice. Under this moonlight.

Then, we need to open the shutters, says the Second Voice.

Yes, says the First Voice. We can open them.

We can't, says the Second Voice.

Why? asks the First Voice.

Because the cold would come in and —

Right, says the First Voice.

And maybe the wolves, says the Second Voice.

Right, says the First Voice. Then: In this case we can only listen.

They listen.

They listen to their own voices.

Outside sounds.

And all the silence (such as).

Some days, begins the First Voice, on a wall I see thousands of faces.

On which wall? says the Second Voice.

On any wall, says the First Voice. After a short pause: On every wall.

On the thick stone walls here? says the Second Voice.

On the dry stone walls here, on the cob walls. On the brick, concrete walls. On all the walls, says the First Voice.

There are no concrete walls here, says the Second Voice. And the dry stone and cob walls are all covered in snow.

Who is talking about "here"? says the First Voice. I'm talking about the walls in my dreams.

Walls in your dreams? asks (befuddled) the Second Voice.

Do you see walls in your dreams?

Yes, says the First Voice. Stone walls. Ruined walls. Summer walls around which lizards sunbathe, ivies twine, kids play marbles.

Yes? says the Second Voice, to indicate that he waits for the end of the sentence.

Yes (the First Voice repeats this word), yes and I see thousands of faces on each wall.

Are they all human faces? says the Second Voice.

The First Voice, (as if) he hasn't heard the question, continues: And on each face thousands of walls.

On human faces? asks (again befuddled) the Second Voice.

On human faces, says the First Voice.

But here you see noone, says the Second Voice. Almost noone.

Does it matter? says the First Voice. My dreams are full of humans.

They remain silent for a while.

After a long while, What do you want? asks the Second Voice.

Nothing, says the First Voice.

Then why're you shouting? says the Second Voice.

I'm not shouting, says the First Voice.

Not now, just a little while ago, says the Second Voice. You shouted just a little while ago. You screamed.

Possible, says the First Voice. I was asleep.

Did you see a dream? says the Second Voice.

Yes, says the First Voice.

Tell it, provided that you don't talk about the walls, says the Second Voice.

Not the walls, says the First Voice. Not the walls this time. I saw a human in my dream. A lonely human. A human being, a humankind. I killed him. I woke up after killing him.

Blood would void dreams they say, says the Second Voice.

I stabbed the knife right in his neck. Blood squirted. And my victim began to shout. At that moment I woke up.

At that moment you must've shouted, says the Second Voice.

I don't remoment, says the First Voice. Maybe you heard the scream of the victim?

Don't talk nonsense, says the Second Voice. Who else could kill & be killed in one's dream but one's self?

I don't understand, says the First Voice.

The Second Voice explains: In your dream you can be the one who kills, but he, I mean your victim, I mean the one killed, with whose voice could he shout?

With his own voice of course, says the First Voice.

How could that be? says the Second Voice. Is there another within yourself? You're the one that saw the dream. He, I mean your victim, I mean the one killed, I mean the one you killed, is a dream being, I mean one who can only be in your dream, I mean, more precisely, a non-being being.

But he shouted, says the First Voice.

Possible, says the Second Voice. But only you can hear his scream. I, on the other hand, can only hear your scream.

Right, says the First Voice. I never thought of that.

Who was the person you killed?

I don't know him, says the First Voice.

Maybe someone you killed in reality? says the Second Voice.

In reality? says the First Voice. Why should I kill someone in reality?

Who knows? says the Second Voice. He remains silent for a while. Then: Maybe you're hiding here because you killed someone?

I'm not hiding or anything, says (harshly) the First Voice. How did you come up with this?

Then, why're you here? says the Second Voice.

And you? says the First Voice.

Because you're here, says the Second Voice.

Right, says the First Voice.

What're we doing here? says the Second Voice. Here on this mountaintop?

We're resting, says (sarcastic) the First Voice.

A special resting, says the Second Voice.

Yes, says the First Voice. Specially prepared for us.

You can't say they don't think about us, says the Second Voice.

They think about us indeed, says the First Voice.

They think all the way up to our wolves, dogs, & dungs, says the Second Voice.

And our substances, says (laughing) the First Voice. They both laugh.

When will the exile be over? says the Second Voice.

I don't know, says the First Voice. Uncertain yet. Soon, I suppose.

In fact, we're not in a condition to whine about, says the Second Voice. What do you say?

Exactly the opposite, says the First Voice. We should be thankful for being sent here.

Yes, says the Second Voice. We have a grass mattress underneath. Three pieces of dung in our stove. And two pieces of flat bread coming from the headman's house everyday.

We may not have had even this, says the First Voice.

Right, says the Second Voice.

A room without a stove for example, says the First Voice.

A room without walls even, says the Second Voice.

No, not that much, says the First Voice.

Or without a roof, says the Second Voice.

Especially without a stove, says the First Voice.

That was said, says the Second Voice.

Right, says the First Voice. He remains silent for a while then adds: Rusty.

What is rusty? asks the Second Voice.

Stove et cetera, says the First Voice.

What's with this pessimism, says the Second Voice.

And with holes, rotten and un-repairable, says the First Voice.

Sure, says the Second Voice. Who knows how many people used it before us. We should be thankful to find even this.

Who could've used it? says the First Voice.

Before us, says the Second Voice. The one who brought this here. Some people like us.

Some people specially sent here on exile you mean, says the First Voice.

I didn't mean that, says the Second Voice.

You mean they drilled the holes in the pipes? says the First Voice.

Which pipes? says the Second Voice.

Water pipes, says the First Voice.

They laugh.

Then, the Second Voice asks, it's reeking, right?

As long as there's something to burn, it can reek, says the First Voice.

We have our dung, says the Second Voice.

We burnt them all, says the First Voice. We don't have dung or dang.

What're we going to burn tomorrow? asks (worried) the Second Voice.

The snow, says the First Voice.

You wren, says the First Voice.

Who? says the Second Voice.

You, says the First Voice. Since you're pensively thinking.

I'm not thinking, says the Second Voice. I remain silent. If I were to think, I'd talk.

Why're you silent? says the First Voice. To kill me; to make me mad?

I was silent, says the Second Voice. Now I'm talking.

What're you talking about, who're you talking to, if you were to talk I'd hear, says the First Voice.

To myself, says the Second Voice.

What're you thinking about? Since you're talking, since you're talking even if only to yourself, even if you're talking from within yourself, goddammit, what're you thinking about? says the First Voice.

About many things, says the Second Voice.

In the meantime? says the First Voice.

Simultaneously?

About many unrelated things, in the meantime, simultaneously, yes, says the Second Voice.

Tell it, says the First Voice. As if thinking. As you think.

How to begin?
Where to begin?
The tough thing is to begin.
While talking. While thinking. While writing.

How to begin? Because I don't know from where to begin. Because I don't know where, when I've begun.

Then how to begin? With which words? With which words, which wouldn't betray me, which I won't have to look for to find, which will be on the tip of my tongue? On impulse? (Which one?) With a pulse? (Which one?) As remembered? (Which one?) As reminded? (Which one?)

Since you want me to tell, whether I want to or not, I'll tell. Since I can't help but telling (to myself or to others), then I'll tell. By necessity. My tongue is the cause of my sufferings. That I know. And yet again:

I'm at a riverside town…

No, no, not this.

Not a tragic ending.

At least not today.

Maybe I've even told this. At another place. Another time. I was in a room. Others were in the room as well. Many others. Crowded.

The room had stone walls. Damp. Moreover without windows. Thus dark. Maybe the room of a mosque. Or a

church. Doesn't matter. Obviously a sanctuary. I don't remoment if the room was already empty, or got emptied
later. Suddenly, in this dark room, we ended up being three
people. An executioner, me, and also… I don't know. The
executioner shows the yataghan. Who is the victim? Me?
The person you couldn't identify? He should be the one.
Then who am I? A witness (as always)? The executioner
continuously looks at me, then to him. He is a muscular
executioner. His hair is oily. His body, too. Because he is
naked. The victim became definite. The executioner came
to me and asked me to tie the victim's hands. I said, I can't.
I'm here by coincidence. I've never helped an executioner.
How could you even want this from me?

The executioner went to the victim. Put your head on
this log, he said. The victim said, Don't behead me. I don't
like blood. If I have to die (and as I see, I have to), hang
me. The executioner said, No. The victim said, Don't I even
have the right to choose the way I die? The executioner
looked at me: You will make a decision, he said. Am I going to make a decision? I said. What decision? I'm not a
judge. I'm here by coincidence (as I told you just a little
while ago), only as a spectator. The executioner said, The
spectators make the decisions nowadays. I cannot decide,
I said. If you want me to decide, I forgive this man, I said.
You forgive him? he said. Who are you to forgive? he said. I
forgive, I said. I forgive as a spectator. Then you undertake
his crime, he said, coming toward me.

I don't know how I slipped away from his hands, found the door, got out & ran away. I ran without looking back. Without looking right or left. When I arrived at the grave-yard, I slowed down. I was breathless. It was just before sunrise. I saw a silhouette just a little further away. I approached. The thorns were twining around my legs. Suddenly, just under my nose, a shovel appeared before me, and a voice: Did you come to help me?

Dead or alive, first I couldn't understand. I was speech-less. Are you his relative? he said. Whose? I couldn't say. I turned my eyes to the sky. The morning stars seen here & there were fading away. A weird light (the light before sunrise) was illuminating where I was. Are you afraid? said the man with a shovel. There's no reason to be afraid. If you're not his acquaintance, & not a sleepwalker who hap-pens to be passing by, if you're the one who slipped away from the executioner's hands, say it, so I get tired no more. I nodded yes. He came out of the pit, which he dug all the way up to his waist. He put his hand on my shoulder. (He left his axe & shovel in the pit.)

Shame, he said. I was digging a nice pit for you. In the best part of the graveyard. A comfortable pit. Now tell me, how did you slip away from the hands of the gypsy?

Finished? says the First Voice.

This was the first chapter, says the Second Voice.

Such a disgusting story, says the First Voice. Such a meaningless story. Don't you dare continue.

However you like, says the Second Voice. You wanted me to tell.

They remain silent.
Resentful (as if).

I will have a story to tell, says the First Voice.
What're you waiting for? says the Second Voice.

I want to edit & summarize it, says the First Voice.

To edit and summarize? says the Second Voice. I hope you won't tell me that you're a writer.

No, never, says the First Voice.

Then what will you edit and summarize? The time of editing and summarizing has passed. Tell it the way it is. Tell it messily. Tell it the way it comes on the tip of your tongue. Tell it the way it passes through your mind.

What I'll tell is not a dream like yours. Not a noise either, says the First Voice.

Whatever it is, says the Second Voice. Tell it the way it is. Tell it how it is.

So hard to tell, says the First Voice.

I know. Be it so. Tell it, says the Second Voice.

I'd never seen her, says the First Voice. I'd only been hearing the noises she'd been making. Her footsteps. All noisy things. I was living on the fifth floor back then, you would remoment. We had two rooms. One kitchen. And a bathroom, too. She was living on the sixth floor. In an attic. In a single room. Her bathroom was outside. Her kitchen was one of the corners of the room. Because of the noises she was making, I got to know where she placed her bed, where her table was set, when she was changing the location of her rocking chair.

Only these? says (laughing) the Second Voice.

Don't interrupt, so I can tell, says the First Voice.

Tell, says the Second Voice. Tell it. I'm listening.

What'll I tell? says the First Voice. I've told it already.

Be it so, continue, says the Second Voice. Or tell something else. Anything. Something nonsensical.

Why? says the First Voice.

To spend time, says the Second Voice. To kill time.

The First Voice tells:

I understood later that the noises she was making weren't pointless.

Each noise, each sound, had significance. The noise she was making when alone in her room was different than the noise she was making when there was someone with her. When someone was in her room, she was telling me through the noises she was making: I'm not alone, there's someone in my room, we'll make love soon. We begin to make love. Lovemaking is over. When she was alone in her room she would stride through the room from one end to the other, and through the sound of her footsteps she was telling me: I'm alone, I'm alone. I'm bored, I'm bored. I would sit down before my typewriter, I would write hitting the keys faster than usual: Alone. I'm alone. I'm bored, I'm bored. I'm bored, I'm writing. She would stop walking upon hearing the tick-tocks of the typewriter. I suppose she'd listen. I suppose she'd understand. It would become deadly quiet, upstairs (her floor), I would say: She went out of her room, is coming down, will come down, will knock on the door, will ask: What're you writing like this? Why this fast? I can't stand it upstairs. As soon as the tick-tocks of my typewriter stop, her walks would begin. She'd say: Your writing is over? Or, you stopped to take a breath? The noises she was making were at times metallic (I was not able to stand those). At times wooden. At times she'd tell that she was bored; at times how happy she was with her life. At times she'd call me (I wouldn't go). At times she'd want me to call her (I wouldn't). At times she'd tell that the man in her bed was useless (the sounds coming out of the spring bed). At times she'd convey how joyful her mating was (the creaking of the spring bed, then the sound of falling on the floor, moaning, shouting, stomping the wooden floor with their feet ...).

At times she'd become deadly quiet, she'd want me to make a noise. At times she'd want me to keep quiet and listen to her. The noises she was making were at times peaceful. At times enraging. But always respectful. She'd make a noise & if she wouldn't receive a response from me, she'd stop the noise. At times she'd walk barefoot on the floor (maybe all naked, especially on summer days, when that heavy, unbearable, temple throbbing, sweaty hot air hovers over the town), at times with her high-heeled shoes. At times she'd even remove the carpet from the floor. She'd walk slowly, all naked, in the void she loves, she has given herself to, really has given, closing her eyes in the void, in the dark void she has fallen. She was a great master of noise. It has to be admitted.

Weird relationship.

Weird relationship, right.

Then?

That is then.

How long did this weird relationship go on, this relationship with no ending?

Until moving out.

Who moved out?

She did, of course.

Ah, see, this I don't remoment.

Maybe that day, you weren't home.

Maybe it was you who moved out.

No, no. She was the one who moved out.

Are you sure?

Since I stayed there. Since I lived there until I came here.

See, this I don't remoment.

You weren't home. If it was me that moved out, you'd remoment, wouldn't you?

Right, says the Second Voice. But I can't remoment anything about this subject.

If you can't remoment, says the First Voice, shut up. He remains silent for a moment. Then: You know it too well: I moved out of that apartment, years after her.

Did anyone else move in to her place? asks the Second Voice, trying to remoment.

No, noone moved in. That room stayed empty until I moved out.

Weird, says the Second Voice.

What's weird? says the First Voice.

That the room stayed vacant for years, says the Second Voice.

Who said that it stayed vacant? says the First Voice.

You, says the Second Voice.

I only said that she moved out. Maybe I said it wrong. I should've said that one day she walked away?

What does this mean? says the Second Voice.

Maybe she left her stuff behind, says the First Voice.

Maybe she went on a journey, you mean? says the Second Voice.

Possible, why not? says the First Voice.

If it was so, say it was so, says the Second Voice.

But I saw her moving out. You also saw it. We came across her on the stairs. She had her luggage. Don't you remoment? says the First Voice.

I saw dozens of people with luggage on the stairs. Which one was she, how could I know; how could I remoment? says the Second Voice.

Is it possible that you forgot? says (befuddled) the First Voice. How could such moments be forgotten?

What kind of moments? says (again befuddled) the Second Voice.

The moments when the noises are over, says the First Voice.

But noises have never been over, says the Second Voice. Even here they go on.

Right, says the First Voice. You're right about this.

They remain silent
— ?

a page.
(meaning quiet)
empty
which should be turned
of a broken-scattered life
Yes

turn the page.
please without thinking any more
Reader,

Don't torture me, says the First Voice.
Don't torture. This is all I wish from you.

Who is torturing? says the Second Voice.

Don't torture me, repeats the First Voice. Don't torture with your questions, your silences, your gazes.

Speak. Tell. Dream. But don't torture.

Are you weary? says the Second Voice. Did I make you feel weary finally? This, have I achieved?

I'm weary of your tortures, says the First Voice.

My silence is torture. My talk is torture. What do you want me to do? says the Second Voice.

I can't stand it anymore, says the First Voice.

We're sitting in here killing time, says the Second Voice. We're waiting for the time to pass.

Are you calling this, killing time? says the First Voice.

Everyone has a way to kill time, says the Second Voice. This is ours.

Yes, says the First Voice. And ours is this torture.

Name it how you want, says the Second Voice. You're the one experiencing this condition. And you're the one to name it. But, I would rather you find a new name for it. A completely new name.

Torture, I say, because you have perpetual questions, says the First Voice.

I was talking about the questions without answers, says the Second Voice. Maybe all of them make a single question.

Yes, says the First Voice. That's why I can't find an answer.

We should've learned long ago that we'd never be able to find an answer, says the Second Voice.

Then why're you asking? says the First Voice. Why're you repeating? Why're you keeping me up at night? Why're you diligently, relentlessly, tirelessly asking me the same question?

My question is mine, says (certain) the Second Voice. I've never posed a question to you. You internalized my questions.

And thus began the torture, says the First Voice.

And thus it will go on, says the Second Voice.

Why? says the First Voice.

Or else would you like to run away? says the Second Voice.

I'd like to, says the First Voice. But I know that there's nothing I can do.

Then there's nothing else we can do, says the Second Voice.

Go on —

We're going on, says the First Voice.

What do you want me to do? says the First Voice.

I want you to talk a little more, says the Second Voice.

Wasn't it enough? says the First Voice.

Not yet, says the Second Voice.

What should I tell? says the First Voice.

Anything. Everything, says the Second Voice.

So hard, says the First Voice.

I know, says the Second Voice. But it's worth trying.

You mean to work our memory? says the First Voice.

Yes, says the Second Voice. Our scabbed memory.

I don't remoment anything, says the First Voice. I can't remoment anything important. Things I remoment are all broken.

As if through the cracks, says the Second Voice.

I remoment, as if leaking, right, says the First Voice. Or broken off. Or broken down. However you like?

If you think these would bring forth an answer, you're mistaken, says (again) the First Voice.

No, says the Second Voice. But it can bring forth clarity to the question. Then: It's fine if it can't.

This effort helps work the memory, says the First Voice.

At least, says the Second Voice.
And the brain, says the First Voice.
No doubt.
It gives rise to thought. It compels thought.
No doubt.
About the things wanted to be thought.
Compellingly.
Compellingly and in complexity.
It has no order undoubtedly.
And no filter.
When it has no method.
In some cases.
Yes.
What are they?
If we were to give examples:
Some people — whose names are forgotten.
What else?
Some names — whose names, forgotten.
What else?
Some people — escaped.
What else?
Some people — dead.
What else?
Some animals — domestic.
What else?
Some plants — ripped or wilted.
What else?
Some houses — collapsed.

What else?

Some ships — sank or ran ashore.

What else?

Some bodies — loved.

What else?

Some words — written.

Aren't there any conversations, any memories, living in its wholeness, unbroken? That can be re-experienced now, at this moment?

Generally broken, says the First Voice.

What's broken? asks the Second Voice.

Not even definite, says the First Voice. Each one of them is broken off. Each one of them is broken into pieces. Each one of them is in their own loneliness. Each one of them is in their own darkness. Each one of them is in their own forgotten-ness.

But they're still living, says the Second Voice.

No doubt, says the First Voice. Their own lives. For example, a woman breastfeeding her baby. But who? Where? When? (I'd recognize her if I see her, but I know that I won't see her again. We know this, right? That I won't see her again. The same image. What I saw today I won't see tomorrow? That we won't be able to see?)

You're talking about the gaps right? says the Second Voice. The gaps you cannot fill.

You've nothing in its wholeness, says (again) the Second Voice; you have it all in pieces, isn't it so?

Yes.

Broken off of a whole, broken into pieces, cannot form a new bond with what it has broken off of, cannot gather & recreate that whole, these are the things that live within you, right?

Cannot create, cannot form, yes, says (as if defeated) the First Voice. But if we were to explain, thus: a whole, broken up, some of its pieces have vanished, only some pieces remain. Or a useless (almost) single piece. Can a whole be formed with it? Based on it, can a whole be remomented? Recreated?

I suppose not, says the Second Voice.

Neither do I, says the First Voice. There are scents I remoment, as parts of that whole, today, at the moment, at any moment I want, living within me.

What kinds of scents? asks (curiously) the Second Voice.

For example, the scent of a river — dried.

A plant, a flower scent — wilted.

An animal scent — dead.

A human scent. A home scent.

A water scent — low tide.

An armpit scent — kissed.

A human scent — smelt.

Such exhaustion, says the Second Voice.

Of the scents? says the First Voice. Hah, I wouldn't trade it for any comfortable mattress.

What about the scent of the get-downs on those comfortable mattresses? says the Second Voice.

And the scent of those get-ups? says the First Voice.

And the get downs-ups? says the Second Voice.
And the get ups-downs? says the First Voice.
And the get ups-downs-ups? says the Second Voice.
Of youth, of our young age, of our youthfulness, you
mean, says the First Voice.

They laugh.

At the words?
At the vanished youth?

They laugh.

The days you hit the road, says the Second Voice, do you remoment?

I hit the road many times, says the First Voice. Which time are you talking about?

About the days when you pushed yourself from one town to another, finding peace in none, says the Second Voice.

From where did this come up, all of a sudden like this, at my place of exile? says the First Voice.

From nowhere, says the Second Voice. From memory.

What is it that comes up from that disgusting memory? asks the First Voice.

The Second Voice explains:

You

going from there to there

didn't know where

going only for the sake of going

thinking you would find relief on the road, on the go

hoping you would find relief by going

you forgot that great saying (the one you recalled often, in your youth)

"You think you can run away from yourself by running away from your land." What was it that you ran away from? If you ask me, you didn't even know. You were just on the road. By yourself. Or with a female by you. By two selves. Hustle and bustle (— Where should we spend this summer? — Wherever you like. — On a mountain top? — No, on the seaside.) The sea was your old passion. The sea and the sun. You wanted to surrender your body to the sun. To think of nothing. To melt away under the sun. To empty your insides. To dissolve. To tan; to eat as much as your hunger; to drink as much as your thirst; to make love as much as your might.

Yes.

Do you remember that trip of ours? You should remoment. It was as if a honeymoon. (Maybe it was a honeymoon, the first & the last.)

The month must have been July.

After a long night trip, you reached a border town.

The female by you: It's beautiful here. Ebb and flow, low & high tides. The sun. Let's not go any further. Let's not get more tired.

You: I can't stay at the borders. Let's continue.

Traveling all day long in the burning hot weather, changing trains, getting on & off the trains, you've finally reached that nasty, ruined town by the river.

You were so tired that you had entered the first hotel you came across. It had one available room. A huge room. With a suite (ha-ha-ha). The area on the side (again huge) was a bathroom. You pulled down the iron shutters. In rooms, all along, you loved dimness.

You turned on the bathroom taps, you got undressed. You also undressed her.

The water filling the tub was ice cold.

When you got into the tub, a noise came from the hot water tap, followed by some steam, then the boiling water flowed out.

She got into the tub only after the water got warmer.

Your lovemaking began in the bathroom, ended on the silky sheets over the large bed.

I remoment as if today, a pink, embroidered, silk sheet it was, that had the warmth of the sun which entered the room through the windows. When you lay on your back, done, you saw the Andalusian engraving on the ceiling first.

Then because of the exhaustion of the trip and the lovemaking and the bath you fell asleep.

When you woke up, you were so hungry. You remomented your hunger. The one near you was sleeping (all naked).

You woke her up.

Let's go & feed ourselves.

You dressed up and left the hotel.

You went to one of the diners on your way.

Things you ordered were: pan fried squid, Cuban style rice, salad, and a dewy bottle of rosé.

You ate the food quickly and got out of there.

The poor kids of the town surrounded you when you got out.

CASTRO ... CASTRO they were yelling at you.

You didn't understand what they meant.
You dropped your tired comrade off at the hotel room.
You wanted to see the town.
You started to walk along the river.
The river (yellow, dirty water) was flowing slowly toward the ocean. Along the coast there were dirty factories with broken windows & a nasty smell.
For a moment
You saw a corpse.
A corpse, taken by the flow of the river, floating away.
A huge dog corpse.
Or some other animal.
I don't know.
All I know is that it was a corpse.
And that it caught your eye —
Traveling along the heavy flow of the river.
You left that town quickly.
When you woke up you said to the one near you:
Come on, prepare the luggage, let's get away.
To where?
Wherever.
Is there a train? Did you ask?
No. But even so, let's go.
There was a train. Going to the south.
You got on.
And in that unbearable hot weather
Watching
Fruitless trees

One-story whitewashed houses
Priests, priest-school students
Donkeys and villagers on donkeys
Whitewashed churches
You began going south.

You were breathing like a person with a weak heart.

The one near you, I don't know what book she was reading.

You didn't open your mouth to say a word until the night fell, until the train reached the last town that it should. Only spoke from within yourself (as you always do, in such situations).

You said to yourself:
Why did I get to this trip
without a plan
a map
a compass?

Do you remoment that town? says the Second Voice.
Of course, says the First Voice.

There, you relentlessly experienced a civil war, says the Second Voice.

Yes, says the First Voice. My own civil war.

But there, the marks of their civil war were also present. The ones that arrived later on, the ones that prevailed, did everything they could to eliminate those marks. But still, they couldn't achieve it. It was apparent far and wide. On the walls. On the ruined buildings. On the people's faces. Their talks.

Yes, says the First Voice. Before I went there, we read about it in books, listened to it on records.

But you hadn't experienced those days in person. You wouldn't know, says the Second Voice.

How? says the First Voice.

You weren't born back then. Or you were just born. You didn't yet know how to write, read.

You know it that way, says the First Voice. I was born long before. As always, I was born. I learned to talk, to read, to write, long before you. Thus, to ask questions. Why are they killing one another? Why here, am I—?

Weird, says the Second Voice. I didn't know you were that old. How old are you really? I'm asking your real age.

My real age, says the First Voice. My real age? You're the one asking me this? I must be very old. I don't know my real age. Just like my mother. But I must be very old.

Unbelievable, says the Second Voice. You don't show it at all.

I'm hiding it, says the First Voice. I'll show my age when I die.

Eh, then we'll learn soon, says (sarcastic) the Second Voice.

Not as soon as you suppose, says the First Voice. I have many days yet to live.

Such weird weather that town had, right, says the Second Voice.

Muggy, says the First Voice.

Deadly, says the Second Voice.

Scorching, says the First Voice.

How you lived in that town, even today I can't understand, says the Second Voice.

In the hotel, in that dim hotel room, says the First Voice.

Yes, says the Second Voice. You found your woman there.

She found that hotel. Came & settled there before you. Told you the address. You called her once you got off the train. She was waiting at the hotel for you. The hotel was not so far away. On the way, while sweating abundantly, you thought about the civil war.

Yes, says the First Voice. You remoment well. Two civil wars. One from the past, one on that day.

When you got to the hotel, first you went up to room 13 on the first floor. Opened the door without knocking. She, in the bed, all naked, was waiting for you. You didn't say anything. You put your luggage aside, undressed, washed your face & hands at the sink.

She: Take a shower if you want; there is a shower on the side.

You: No need.

With all your tiredness, all your sweat, all your desire, you throw yourself on her nakedness.

The First Voice laughs. Such a scent that was, he says. The scent of the hotel; the scent of sweat; the scent of summer lovemaking. Alongside all, the scent of gunpowder.

The scent of gunpowder? says the Second Voice. From where did that come up?

Throughout my stay in that town, I sensed the scent of gunpowder, says the First Voice.

The guns were however quieted a long time ago, says the Second Voice.

Yes, says the First Voice. But again the scent of gunpowder remained in the air. Was it Africa?

No, I suppose not, says the Second Voice. People on the streets were rather white. Like you and me. Almost.

Right, says the First Voice. Maybe I'm mistaken. Maybe I got confused. Right, can't be Africa.

What caused your confusion? says the Second Voice.

Maybe the female near me, says the First Voice.

Is that possible? says the Second Voice. She wasn't black.

Who says so? says the First Voice. Maybe we're talking about different things? Who was the one waiting for me in the hotel room of that hot town if not a black woman?

Could you be so forgetful? says the Second Voice. In all your life you slept with one black person and only once. Where and how it was, you should remoment well. Because it was unforgettable.

Maybe I forgot, says the First Voice. You tell me about that town. That female. That me.

A white, blonde female, she was. After you made love, you went to the shower on the side and washed. A cold shower helped you to get back to yourself. Then you shaved, went back in the room, and said that you would leave & wander around.

She: By yourself?

You: Yes.

She: You can't go out at this time. It's deadly hot. Wait, for the sunset.

You: I want to wander around in the heat. Under the sun.

She: This is not the kind of sun you know of. It would hit. It would kill.

You: Let's try and see.

You tried.

In the human-less town you wandered around from there to there; sweating a lot; drinking cold stuff in the open cafes you found.

Around sunset you met her in a café. An open-air café. You got there before her. There was a newspaper in front of you. A newspaper of a place whose language you don't know. You were reading as if you knew. When she came, you put down the newspaper, told her about your trip, then asked:

Did you see the marks of the civil war?

I watch them on your face, she said, marks of a real civil war. On your face, in your eyes.

She watched for a long time.

Until being done with it.

Was that a philosopher, who said this? Or a psychologist? Or a sociologist? Or a whore? asks the First Voice.

I forget, says the Second Voice.

Do you remember that night? says the First Voice.

Which night? asks (this time) the Second Voice.

The naked night when we, all together (you, me, him, us, you, them), according to our customs, lay down on the rugs over the floor.

The night when deerskins were thrown over us, and with our females by us?

Yes, says the First Voice.

Don't remind, says the Second Voice.

You weren't able to hold your tongue there either, says the First Voice.

Where have I ever been able to hold it, anyway, says the Second Voice.

But you should have held it there, says the First Voice.

Don't remind, says the Second Voice.

I have to remind, every now & then, says the First Voice. The word 'remind' and the tests you've taken.

I said don't remind, says the Second Voice.

Not only your tongue, but you couldn't hold your lower back also, if I'm not mistaken, says the First Voice.

I could never hold it, says the Second Voice. Do I need to lie? It wasn't in my hands. I can't hide what god knows from the serf. From you, them, and me; I can hide from noone.

Well, you couldn't hold your lower back here either, says the First Voice.

Don't remind, says the Second Voice.

What should I not remind of, it happened just yesterday, says the First Voice.

Don't remind me of yesterday, says the Second Voice.

What about what happened just now? says the First Voice.

Don't remind me of now either, says the Second Voice.

When will you disappear? says the First Voice.

When the frost melts, says the Second Voice.

When the flesh separates from the bone.

When the bones rot, disintegrate.

When the memory blows in the wind.

When mother earth dries out.

When the memories disappear.

Which means, never, says the First Voice.

No, it's close at hand, says the Second Voice.

Your hand, says the First Voice.

How clever you are, says the Second Voice.

Shall we let go of the old days, what do you say? says the First Voice.

No problem for me, says the Second Voice.

Shall we look at the rising day? says the First Voice.

We look at it every morning, says the Second Voice.

Shall we learn from what's happened, what's passed, what do you say? says the First Voice.

I'm ready, says the Second Voice.

In this case, do you know what we'll talk about? says the First Voice.

No, says the Second Voice. About everything. Maybe. About nothing. Maybe.

Maybe about a dream, says the First Voice.

Unseen, says the Second Voice.

Maybe about a fact, says the First Voice.

Unheard of, says the Second Voice.

Maybe about us, says the First Voice.

Not enough? says the Second Voice.

Maybe about them, says the First Voice.

Why not? A must, says the Second Voice.

Maybe about nothing, says the First Voice.

Maybe about silence, says the Second Voice.

Maybe about the air, says the First Voice.

Maybe about the water, says the Second Voice.

Never, says the First Voice.

Then let's choose, says the Second Voice.

Choose what? says (befuddled) the First Voice.

Our subject, says the Second Voice.

Our subject? says (befuddled) the First Voice. Didn't we choose our subject? Years ago?

But, says the Second Voice. We always revolve around the same subject.

What else can we do? says the First Voice.

Some change, some color, says the Second Voice.

All is included in our subject, says the First Voice.

Right, says the Second Voice.

Human, says the First Voice.

Human, human beings you said? says the Second Voice.

I haven't said anything, says the First Voice.

Then he remains silent.

He gets up from where he lies. Goes in front of the window. The day is almost set. Snow and snow. Nothing else. On the hills across, here and there, some trees bursting out of the snow. Eye-tiring whiteness.

He brings the shutters of the window down.

Enough! Enough!

Enough talking! Enough silence!

To work the memory!

To dream.

To see a dream.

Constant exhaustion.

We came here. This mountaintop. Again, it isn't over.

Enough is enough!

He goes back to the bed again. Lies down.

He holds his breath.

Deadly quiet. (He seeks quiet even in this quietude.)

He listens to his heartbeats.

His eyes shut.

Behind his eyelids: An infinite room.

The walls are covered with rugs and carpets. Among them are some old gilded frames. Istanbul-crafted. With unidentifiable pictures inside. Some have writings on them.

On the corner somewhere hung a hand mill. On the floor, set side by side, are different sizes and types of pestles (bronze, wood, marble ... Roman, Selchuk, Ottoman, Italian ...), in the middle, a long table. Solid oak. Style: Renaissance. Type: English. A chandelier hangs from the ceiling. Crystal. Dusty. Unlit.

He moves forward. On the carpet, wet footprints. In front of him, a sofa. With a very high back. Covered with velvet. He approaches this sofa. He approached. Leaning over the sofa. There is a woman. She has long blonde hair, covering her nudity. Her eyes, shut. Her hair, falling over her chest, wet. She is asleep or not, not clear. Her breath, intermittent.

She didn't hear the footsteps approaching her. Or she heard and pretended she didn't.

He, turning around, comes to the front of the sofa. Sits down on the carpet.

Soft, worn down here & there, old, but keeps its main quality, a Konya carpet.

He holds the woman's hand and pulls it away from between her legs. The woman doesn't open her eyes to look. He puts his head in the middle of her legs. The woman's right hand reaches for the nape of his neck. Her head, leaning on the back of the sofa, turns from left to right (eyes always shut). For a moment her lips move apart. Teeth clench. Moaning begins. They are over the carpet.

When the man gets up, where is my watch? he asks. Where is my watch?

I don't know, the time passed. I forgot my watch somewhere. There is no time. Why is there no time? What happened to time?

But the minutes are counted, seconds are counted. However, (still) it can't be said that there is time. Falling snow is counted. Arriving letters (if they arrive). The radio that is listened to. The news that is received (today in Vietnam... the Middle East war... hunger in Biafra... general strikes in Paris... Johnson's last speech...). Rising sun. Setting sun. Yet another day has passed. We get closer, yet another day. (To what?) Lying down. Getting up. Dreams are seen. Asleep and awake (just like a moment ago).

Whose are the days, hours, minutes?

Lying down. Closing eyes.

But noone sleeps. Dreaming:

An infinite room. The walls are covered with rugs and carpets. Among them, gilded frames. With some ornamented calligraphy, some unornamented scribble...

Tonight, you have no intention to talk, I see, says the Second Voice.

Tonight you want to be alone with your dreams, I see, says the Second Voice.

Tonight, you don't want to continue, I understand, says the Second Voice.

Tonight you want to make love, apparently, says the Second Voice.

Why should I continue? says the First Voice.

To what? says the Second Voice. To live?

Our life here, to talk, says the Second Voice. That's what I meant to say.

Because there's nothing else to do, is that why? says the First Voice.

Why to continue? this I asked, says the Second Voice.

What to continue? says the First Voice. To talk?

No, to write, says the Second Voice.

As you see, we don't have light, says the First Voice. We're out of paraffin. We're in darkness.

That's ok, says the Second Voice. One can also write in darkness.

With illegible handwriting, says the First Voice.

Groping, says the Second Voice.

Do you remoment the days of exile?
says the First Voice.

To remoment? We're experiencing them at the moment, says the Second Voice.

Which one is this? Tell me that, says the First Voice.

I haven't counted, says the Second Voice. But, it should be neither the first nor the last one.

In the north, in a snowy country we once were, I know that, says the First Voice. Then we migrated to a sunny country in the south. We couldn't make it there either. We looked for the sea. We hit the road again, do you remoment? We came by an island.

Why are you constantly remomenting the old days, old exiles? says the Second Voice. Why are you telling me about the old days, old lives? Not over yet?

Why are you getting offended? says the First Voice. All these have a reason. You should know that reason.

What is that reason? Tell me so we learn, says the Second Voice.

To work the memory, says the First Voice.

What do you expect to gain by this? says the Second Voice.

Nothing, says the First Voice. What've we gained up until today? To gain what we've worked for? I don't expect anything. But still I can say —

But still you can say what? says (angry) the Second Voice.

Better than nothing, I can say, says the First Voice. In this room, on this mountaintop, during the closure of these roads, during the absence of the mail, yet still better than nothing, I can say.

What is better? says the Second Voice.

To remoment. To work the memory, says the First Voice.

Right, says the Second Voice.

North … Snowy country, says the First Voice.

South … Sun, says the Second Voice.

West, humid region, says the First Voice.

Northwest, foggy town, says the Second Voice.

Sun, sea, island, says the First Voice.

Mediterranean? says the Second Voice.

Maybe Spain, maybe Portugal, maybe Syphilis, says the First Voice.

You know well that I've never messed with it, says the Second Voice.

Thank god, says the First Voice. But there was no reason for you not to mess with it.

You're right, says the Second Voice.

You did all you could, to survive, says (sarcastic) the First Voice.

Whose fault? says the Second Voice.

Probably mine, says the First Voice. I exiled you from there to there.

All my exiles were voluntary, says the Second Voice.

This time, too? says the First Voice.

All of them, says the Second Voice.

One day you'll tell me about them, will you? says the First Voice.

When I've nothing left to tell, maybe, says the Second Voice.

When you've run out of, you meant to say? says the First Voice.

That's what I meant, says the Second Voice.

Then you can start as soon as tomorrow, says (again sarcastic) the First Voice.

Time is not passing, says the First Voice.
Why do you want it to pass? says the Second Voice.

To get old, says the First Voice.

Time is passing, says the Second Voice. Moreover, all by itself. Don't tire yourself much about this subject.

I can't hear it passing here, says the First Voice. As if, with everything else, time is also paused.

Maybe it is paused. Maybe every time is paused. What is it to you?

Days are being counted, says the First Voice. Hours are being counted. How come, what is it to me?

Make time flow faster then, if you're this interested, says the Second Voice. Not to feel its weight over you. It's in our hands.

How? says the First Voice.

By telling, by referring to the old days, by thinking about the future, says the Second Voice.

You suppose it'd be of any help? says the First Voice.

I can't see any other way out, says the Second Voice. Especially when we're under these conditions.

Then speak, tell, but tell me about the future only, says the First Voice.

To tell about the future, says the Second Voice. It's necessary to remoment yesterday, & to put today into words.

Then remain silent, shut up, says the First Voice. At least tonight.

No, says the Second Voice. You started. I will continue. I will tell about the old days. Old lives. Old deaths. Old loves. Old places.

Enough, says the First Voice. I don't feel like listening. Enough.

Whether you listen or not, says the Second Voice. It's nothing to me. I'm talking for myself now.

Great egoist, accuses the First Voice. You were always like this. You've always talked for yourself. You've always told for yourself. You've always lived for yourself. The things you will tell, at least, tell them from within yourself.

I'm talking within myself, already, says the Second Voice. As I always do. Things expressed are my murmurs only. Things expressed are not words. Syllables, at the utmost. The ones I can't prevent.

All can be yours, says the First Voice. Just know this, I won't listen to you tonight.

Whether you want to listen or not, it's up to you, says the Second Voice. I begin:

And begins the Second Voice:

What was the name? — Karakura. — Or can it be Albastı? — No, Çarsambakarısı. — Or maybe Karakanca-loz. — No way, that was Süleyman. — Then this is Albız. — No, Alboz. — Or Cangoloz. — What did it do? — It ſtopped by our home. —

When? — When I was a kid at Doymazdere. — I can remoment, a dark dry cold night it was… the month was, if I'm not wrong, Pederim Cemheri… it came to take you, too… — Who?… — Pederim. — Possible. — I don't know, I was sleeping. — But thank god you didn't go out. Before going out, you woke up. Was that a lesson for you? — I suppose not. — Not at all? — I don't know. I suppose it taught me fear, & to believe in everything. — In everything? — Yes. In Kakkar, in Cettar, in Gaffar, in Evvel, in Ahir, in Aziz, in Samet, & also in Vahid. — You believed in all these? — Yes. All along. How long? Up until a thousand year ago.

All these things you told are over, says the Second Voice.

What's over? says the First Voice.

All these things you told, says the Second Voice. Nonsense. Wild. Selfish. All these things you told. Meaningless. Or their meaning is hidden only in you.

But I haven't told anything yet, says the First Voice.

We know, says (in plural) the Second Voice. All the things you remained silent about. All the things you kept to yourself. All the things you want to tell but couldn't. All the things you will tell (one day). All the things you want to tell but couldn't find the time to. All the things you want to tell but couldn't find the words for. All your efforts. Empty, without an echo. All you.

If so, I have to go away, says the First Voice. If it's so, I should never open my mouth again. And if I open it, I should be far away. Far away from you. It's time to get away from you, if so.

Your wound began to bleed again, apparently, says the Second Voice.

It's never scabbed over, anyway, says the First Voice.

For it to bleed, you don't need to scratch.

Thank god, says the Second Voice. Otherwise it would've been painful for me.

My wound is a carbuncle, says the First Voice. On my chest. On the left side of my chest.

An incurable wound, says (amused) the Second Voice. Maybe a cancer.

Shut up, says the First Voice. Enough is enough. I don't feel like enduring.

Me or your wound? says the Second Voice.

You're the same shit, says the First Voice.

Since what time? says the Second Voice.

Since all of time, says the First Voice.

I didn't know, says the Second Voice.

You should've known, says the First Voice.

Taking your revenge on me, says (resentful) the Second Voice.

Shut up, shouts the First Voice. Shut up. Don't open your disgusting mouth. Don't say a thing. Just listen.

To what? says the Second Voice.

Listen, says the First Voice.

They listen to the howling dogs in the night and the moaning north wind.

While listening, the First Voice continues. (As though) on behalf of both:

Scents of cotton
Times of trees
Whirlpools of the whirling wheels
Like a murmur
Reflect on us.

It is our fate.

As if moaning, the First Voice uttered these weird words. Monotone, but still as if moaning, with rises and falls. As if trying to rip the words out of his larynx. As if maybe a primal, maybe a religious chant.

Like a murmur? says (befuddled) the Second Voice.
Called so, says the First Voice.
So called, fate, yes, says the Second Voice.

They remain silent for a while.

Even the dogs stopped howling.

You know what, you kind of look like humanity, says the First Voice.

Like a human, says the Second Voice. Kind of?

Like humanity, I said, says the First Voice.

What part of me looks like it? says the Second Voice.

Your nature, says the First Voice.

Which nature? says the Second Voice.

Your tranquil days are followed by your worrisome days, says the First Voice.

Is it my fault? says the Second Voice.

However, you get bored of tranquil days & you create the worries yourself.

What else? says the Second Voice.

You want to accomplish something, and once you do, you overthrow it.

Are you talking about the doghouse I made in the garden? Or the snowman I made with the kids yesterday morning on the patio? says the Second Voice.

I'm talking about you, says the First Voice. How many times you overthrew your happiness...

They were not happinesses, says the Second Voice.

How many times you overthrew your beloveds?

They were not my beloveds.

How many times you broke your friendships?

If there were happinesses, my beloveds, friendships, I wouldn't have been here now. At least I wouldn't have been like this.

Comfort pricks our ass, says the First Voice.

You can't say that I've ever experienced comfort.

You were the most comfortable man on earth once, says the First Voice. However, as humanity has wars, you, too, have your own civil war. For that you are forgiven.

Thanks, says the Second Voice.

Where are you? the Second Voice starts to talk. Are you here? If you're here, say yes.

Yes, says the First Voice. I'm here.

Where, here? says the Second Voice.

Here, in my room on this mountaintop. In my dark room on this mountaintop. Alone in here, in my room on this mountaintop. In a tiny corner of this room. Talking to myself. Pouring out my grief to myself. By myself — if you really want to learn.

Who are you deceiving? says the Second Voice.

How? says the First Voice.

There are others, says the Second Voice.

They, too, are here, in my loneliness, says the First Voice.

What're they doing? says (sarcastic) the Second Voice.

They're in here, says the First Voice. (Points to his heart with his hand. But in this darkness noone sees this.) Everyone is in here. The ones outside. The ones inside. The ones far away. The ones close by. You, me, all of us, are in here. All the worries. All the worried.

I can't spot it in the darkness, says (laughing) the Second Voice. Are you showing your heart, or something?

Yes, says (angry) the First Voice. My heart, my brain, my stomach, my groin, my ass, my taint, my balls… Do you want me to continue counting?

Enough, enough, says the Second Voice. Just tell me what they do in there.

They're kneading dough, will roll filo dough, make bread, says the First Voice. Today they're making yogurt. They'll send a bowl of it to you tomorrow. They're throwing a gunny over the kids. Breastfeeding their babies. Stomp-dancing over their wives. Burning the stove. They're under their husbands. Talking in the candlelight. Kissing in the dark.

What're they thinking about in the meantime? the Second Voice continues his question with sarcasm.

Everything and nothing, says the First Voice. They're not thinking about yesterday. They're saying that one doesn't die with the dead. Today is also over, they're saying. Let's see what happens tomorrow, they're saying. Hope the frost will melt so that we won't lose more sheep, they're saying. Winter strung out, they're saying.

What else?

Else, they're thinking about their wives and husbands, their dogs, ovine and bovine animals, barley and wheat-ears, children yet to be born, sheep yet to be born, summer yet to come, zoster. Inside their heads is too confusing, if you knew, if you entered, if you talked to them, you'd say: They're not thinking about anything, they live for the day, they're not thinking about anything, they don't worry about anything, you'd say. You'd suppose they only think of themselves. You wouldn't even suppose that. They just live, you'd say.

And they live, says the Second Voice.

They live of course, says the First Voice.

And you're thinking about them, is it so? says the Second Voice.

About them and myself. About myself and them. No longer differentiating between you, me, he/she/it, them, here, on this mountaintop, knowing that we share the same fate; and saying "we" in my dreams and in my thoughts.

But they are so many, says the Second Voice. And not only here.

They're everywhere, sure, says the First Voice.

And their worries are more than them, says the Second Voice.

Yes, says the First Voice. They're so many. Almost all of humanity, I'd say.

You could say, says the Second Voice.

Do you ever ask yourself: Who was the escapee? says the Second Voice.

Which escapee? Is there anyone escaping? Where? How? When? says (hectic) the First Voice.

I don't know, says the Second Voice. An emotion. A question. Who escaped? From what? From whom? For what? says the First Voice, lining up his questions (again).

I don't know, says the Second Voice. From time to time it feels like I escape from something, am escaping from something, or some people escape from something, are escaping from something, better to say we are escaping altogether. I sense this. As if I'm sensing this. A blurry question. But a question.

Nonsense, a meaningless question, says the First Voice. Everywhere, all the time, there was an escape — there is — there would be.

Right, says the Second Voice. But what're we doing among them?

Because these are of interest to you, says the First Voice.

What, who are the ones you call "these"? says the Second Voice.

Escape, the escapees, says the First Voice.

Right, says the Second Voice. You're right. I've never thought of this subject.

For example, A., says the First Voice.

What is it with A.? says the Second Voice.

He had been escaping from himself, you will remoment, says the First Voice.

B. had been escaping from the world, adds the Second Voice. Now who knows where he is?

Within the world, says the First Voice.

C. also escaped, right, says the Second Voice.

Yes, says the First Voice. He escaped from his wife & children.

D. escaped from the god, says the Second Voice.

That is called, being caught up with the hound while escaping from the rabbit, says (laughing) the First Voice.

Who're you talking about? says (befuddled) the Second Voice.

About D. and god, says the First Voice.

Doesn't understand. Pauses. Then asks as if he understood: Being caught up with the hound while escaping from the rabbit? says the Second Voice.

Hahhahhah-Huhuhuhuhuhuhh… Kah-kah-kah kahkah … they both laugh, holding their groins, at this meaningless saying.

Let's continue, says the Second Voice.

Who were we at? asks (ready) the First Voice.

At D., says the Second Voice.

We said that, says the First Voice. He escaped from the god.

E., says the Second Voice, we know him closely, he escaped from his homeland.

Supposing he'd been rescued, says the First Voice.

No need to comment, says the Second Voice.

F. from military training, says the First Voice.

But then, he surrendered, says the Second Voice.

G., from the prison cell, says the First Voice.

He was sentenced to 30 years. What else could he have done, but escape? says the Second Voice.

No need to comment, says the First Voice.

What was his crime? Do you remoment? says the Second Voice.

He killed someone, I suppose, says the First Voice.

I suppose not, says the Second Voice. If I'm not mistaken he raped someone.

Possible, says the First Voice. He must've killed after raping.

He wasn't the kind of man who would do such things, says the Second Voice. In my opinion, you're mistaking him for someone else.

Then you tell me, says the First Voice.

I think, his crime was political, says the Second Voice.

You're right, says the First Voice. His name was involved in a political murder.

But he escaped right on time, says the Second Voice.

Like all who escaped and found redemption.

Like us, says the Second Voice.

Don't stir us in, says the First Voice.

Up until today he hasn't been caught, right? says the Second Voice.

As far as I know, he wasn't caught, says the First Voice.

Let's continue, says the Second Voice.

Where were we? says the First Voice.

H., says the Second Voice.

H. escaped from a protest, says the First Voice.

Noone must have forced him to this, says the Second Voice.

Noone forced him to, anyway, says the First Voice. He escaped by himself.

Ok, continue, says the Second Voice.

We get to I., he escaped from the hospital, says the First Voice.

Call it an asylum, says the Second Voice.

Like us, says the First Voice.

Noone asked, says the Second Voice.

He hasn't been caught either, says the First Voice.

He hasn't got a thing, poor man, says the Second Voice.

He lost his mind a little like all of us, says the First Voice.

Neither more nor less, says the Second Voice.

His escape proves that, says the First Voice.

J. escaped from the bridal chamber. I remoment this one very well, says the Second Voice.

Me too, says the First Voice.

How would you not remoment; the next day his wife threw herself into your arms.

I consoled her well, you should give me my due, says the First Voice.

I think the most interesting was K., says the Second Voice. None of us know why he escaped from you.

But, we never got to know him, says the First Voice.

And there is also L., says the Second Voice. We never got to know him either, but we heard of him.

From where did he escape? says the First Voice.

I cannot remoment at this moment, says the Second Voice.

Maybe from himself, says the First Voice.

Like many others, says the Second Voice.

We forgot the one who escaped from heaven, says the First Voice.

Don't start the fairy tale, says the Second Voice.

Then can you tell, from where, when, for what, from whom we escaped? says the First Voice.

We? says the Second Voice.

Yes, says the First Voice. Since you want us to be realistic, let's look at ourselves a bit, if you allow.

So we also escaped? says the Second Voice.

You were the one telling that just a little while ago, says the First Voice.

Since others escaped, since everyone escaped, we also must've escaped from something, from somewhere, says the Second Voice.

Where're the others? says the First Voice. I'm curious. We're here. On this mountaintop. All alone.

With this, you mean, we haven't escaped? says the First Voice.

The Second Voice doesn't answer this question.

Did we do a good thing not escaping? says the First Voice.

The Second Voice doesn't answer this question.

Right, we're all alone, says the First Voice.

He receives no response from the Second Voice.

This loneliness, says the First Voice.

What makes us talk, says the Second Voice.

Yes, says the First Voice. Here, now, at this moment, in this room we're alone and we're talking.

What do you want to say? says the Second Voice. Here? Now? At this moment?

What else can I say? says the First Voice.

Why're you talking to yourself? Why're you murmuring by yourself? Why, by yourself, are you lining up the escapees? Why're you grumbling? Why're you chewing the words in your mouth?

Not by myself, says the First Voice. There are thousands of voices. You're one of them. There are thousands of voices that speak. There are thousands of voices that knead me. In here (he points to his head, then his chest), throwing me away, talking about me, making me talk, crying, crying out, dreaming, shouting in their dreams, calling for help, sending me away, cursing, respecting, calling me my darling, telling me to die, running, going down, going up, being infested with lice, being eaten ...

Is that why you talk in the plural? says the Second Voice.

I wish, says (touching) the First Voice.

Speak, says the Second Voice.

What shall I say? says the First Voice. Everything has been said.

Do you suppose? says the Second Voice.

For now, says the First Voice. One day you said that.

Possible, says the Second Voice. But back then we hadn't lived through these days, yet.

What do you want to say? says the First Voice.

On this mountaintop, says the Second Voice, some new things can be said.

For example? says the First Voice.

Say, insists the First Voice. Tell me who I can talk to. Because already I'm weary of talking in a desert.

Say, says the First Voice. Here, on this mountaintop, whose worries can we listen to; who can we tell our worries to? Let's talk, fine, says the First Voice. But we don't even know the language of these people.

Well, we're learning, says the Second Voice.

What we learn are just words, says the First Voice. Do you suppose that would be enough to talk, to tell about your worries, to listen to worries?

For now, says the Second Voice, even more than enough. And — after a long pause he adds: Haven't we always used dry words, always broken words, up until today, in our own language, too?

You might be right, says the First Voice. I've never thought about it.

Maybe I'm mistaken, says the Second Voice. Just you talk; just let's see.

I want to know what's after, says the First Voice.

Just you begin, says the Second Voice. First talk to yourself of course. As you always do.

Shall we do a warm up? says the First Voice.

Yes, says the Second Voice.

Then, says the First Voice.

Then, the mountain, the stones we can talk to, says the Second Voice. Grasses, birds we can talk to. Then we can experience here, we can begin experiencing here; we can understand here, we can begin understanding here; we would talk about here. We would eat their herbed cheeses; we would carry over their folk songs, their pain, their painful folk songs.

We would carry over, says (almost enthusiastic) the First Voice. With words. Both belonging to us and not. With our words.

With our words, yes, says the Second Voice.

Ah, if only the roads were not closed,
begins the First Voice.

Ah, if only there was an unread book, he says, then.

Ah, if only there was a blank piece of paper, he says, after.

Ah, if only there was some more rakı, he says even after.

Ah, if only there was no ah, the Second Voice breaks in.

We're on a mountaintop — don't forget this, says (resentful) the First Voice.

I couldn't forget even if I wanted to, says the Second Voice.

We're alone here, in this room. Don't let this slip away from your mind when talking to me — this is two, says the First Voice.

We're not that alone, especially tonight, says the Second Voice.

Don't look to books for help — this is three, says the First Voice.

You're the one to think about that, says the Second Voice.

Neither to papers and pencils. Nor to the mail. The roads are buried under the snow — this is four, five, and six, says the First Voice.

That is why I wanted you to talk, says the Second Voice.

All rakı has already been drunk, drunkenness has also passed, we have to live sober from now on — this is seven and eight, says the First Voice.

That is why I wanted you to talk, says the Second Voice.

Don't despair of the sun — this is nine, says the First Voice.

Then speak, says the Second Voice.

They remain silent.

Then,

I saw the bone bleeding, says Someone.

I saw the blood flowing, says the Other.

Where have you passed by to get here, to say this? says Someone.

Through many hollows, says the Other.

Such exhaustion, says Someone.

Yes, says the Other.

Such loneliness, says Someone.

Yes, says the Other.

It's almost daybreak, says Someone.

Sunlight hit the mountains across, says the Other.

Reflecting on our window, says Someone.

Of course it will reflect, says the Other.

Of course it will reflect, says the Other.

Of course it will reflect, says Someone and the Other.

One almost wants to say that, says the First Voice.

Yes, says the Second Voice, because that's what should be said.

At times I think … says the First Voice.

What do you think? says the Second Voice, not waiting for the First Voice to finish the sentence.

At times I think, says the First Voice, a departure point has to be found, I say. And at times, I feel like we are on that departure point.

Possible, says the Second Voice. Who knows; maybe that is the case.

One can wait with this thought in mind, says the First Voice.

For what? says the Second Voice.

For the snow to melt, says the First Voice.

The snow? says the Second Voice.

Yes, says the First Voice. To melt.

But we'll need to wait for a long time, says the Second Voice. As you see, it continues to snow.

It's ok, says the First Voice. We'll wait.

For how long? says the Second Voice.

As long as is needed, says the First Voice.

What a change, says the Second Voice.

This is a lake waiting to reach a river, a river waiting to reach a sea, says the First Voice.

Are we going to be able to wait that long, says the Second Voice. We are very far away from the sea here, you know.

I know, so what? says the First Voice.

Are we going to see that day you say? says the Second Voice.

Which day? says the First Voice.

The day of reaching the sea, says the Second Voice.

What does it matter? says the First Voice.

Are you the one saying this, says the Second Voice.

Yes, says (dry and sharp) the First Voice.

What about the snow? says the Second Voice.

It'll melt; it's close at hand, says the First Voice.

But we're not even in old March yet, says the Second Voice.

It's close at hand, says (stubborn) the First Voice.

What's close at hand? says (forgetful) the Second Voice.

The melting of the snow, says the First Voice. Snow to melt flowing in streams, reaching to the lakes, lakes to the rivers, rivers to the sea.

All this snow? says the Second Voice.

And how! says the First Voice. Even the snow on the summit.

And then, says the Second Voice.

And then the flowers will blossom, snowdrops, says (cheerful like a child) the First Voice. You'll see the mountain rabbits, the bears awaken from winter sleep, mountain goats following their offspring, jumping from stone to stone, the opening of the roads connecting men to men, town to town. Then, only then —

Then are we going to go away from here? says the Second Voice.

I don't know, says the First Voice. And I can't think ahead of time.

All right, what're we going to do here? On this mountaintop? What will become of us? says the Second Voice.

We'll continue living where we are, as we are; I mean changing every day, every moment; I mean in constant becoming, says the First Voice. Just as it has been up until today. Maybe longer.

While waiting for that day? says the Second Voice.

While waiting for that day, we'll also talk, argue, learn to wait; we'll wait, says the First Voice.

Yes, says the Second Voice. As long as there's something to wait for.

And then
After a long silence:

But such a horrible winter, such an exhausting, such an unbearable, such an unnerving winter this is, says the Second Voice.

You're right, says the First Voice.

Such a

Long

Difficult

Intricate

Complicated

And cold

And freezing

Weary

Remorseless winter.

You're right.

However we should know how to wait.

Waiting. That is what is hard and unbearable, says the Second Voice.

Patience, says the First Voice. What is expected from us is patience.

What patience? says the Second Voice. Say, give a date.

What date? says (befuddled) the First Voice. What date?

When will the snow melt? When will we go? says the Second Voice.

So soon, says the First Voice.

When is, so soon? says (almost rebellious) the Second Voice.

I suppose very soon, says the First Voice. But I can't give a date.

Probably not tomorrow, says the Second Voice.

Neither the day after, says the First Voice.

Will we see, at least, says the Second Voice.

See what? asks (befuddled or not comprehending the question) the First Voice.

The melting of the snow, unlike yesterday, the rise of the real summer sun? says the Second Voice.

No doubt, says the First Voice. But patience is needed. Learning is needed. To wait. The things to do while waiting. Then, no doubt, you'll see; the sun is close at hand. You know the first sign of spring is here, already.

Where? says the Second Voice. In the air?

No, on the earth, says the First Voice.

We're waiting for the second sign now? says the Second Voice.

Yes, says the First Voice.

So we found something to wait for? says the Second Voice. Something concrete.

It wasn't easy, says the First Voice. The ones after this may be even more difficult.

It's been very difficult for us to reach here, says the Second Voice.

But now we know what we're waiting for, says the First Voice.

Yes, says the Second Voice. The third sign.

Yes, says the First Voice. But — (some whispers which were made inaudible, erased by the wind & the howling of the dogs outside).

It's heard that the Second Voice says, Ok.

And the First Voice says, However you like, I'm telling you.

If I see a frightening dream, says the Second Voice —

Don't worry; I would wake you up, says the First Voice.

Did you think about it? says the Second Voice.

About what? says the First Voice.

About what you will tell, says the Second Voice.

About what I will tell? says the First Voice. Am I to tell something?

Yes, says the Second Voice. You were to tell something. You need to tell something. You have to tell something.

Why? says (befuddled) the First Voice.

To find relief, says the Second Voice.

Right, I remoment, says the First Voice. I was to tell something.

Come on, tell it, says the Second Voice.

I'm thinking, says the First Voice.

Don't think, just tell, says the Second Voice.

I'm looking for it, says the First Voice.

What're you looking for? says the Second Voice.

The words, says the First Voice.

Don't think. Don't look for. Just tell. Begin telling. Words will come out by themselves, says (encouraging) the Second Voice.

But I have to think to begin. The words, I need to find the required words, says the First Voice.

Say the first word that is on the tip of your tongue to begin with, says the Second Voice.

Let's try, says the First Voice. This is a way, too.

And he tries:

A room.

Two people in a room.

Two people in a room, male or female I don't know (pauses).

The Second Voice continues: It doesn't matter if they're male or female.

Two people, continues the First Voice. Two lonely people, on a mountain, in a room on a mountaintop, walls are whitewashed adobe, two sleepless people.

Two people, telling their dreams to one another.

They're telling their made-up stories to one another

Their lives and deaths

They live in yesterday and today together

While dogs are howling outside

Their dreams, their falls, are on this mountaintop

On this cold mountaintop

At this snowy mountaintop

On this lonely mountaintop

I suppose they're alone

On this mountaintop

Maybe there aren't

Two people

Maybe one

Maybe not even one.

What do you want? says the Second Voice.

I told everything, nothing anymore, says the First Voice.

What've you ever wanted and when? says the Second Voice. When've you ever known what you wanted?

Never, says the First Voice. I accept. Never. Maybe. Almost. Not. Ever. Except my hunger and thirst. I can tell openly. But now, at this moment, on this mountaintop, in this room on this mountaintop, there's something that is —

Yes, cuts the Second Voice. I understand. It's time now, you think. You're conscious about it now, you think.

After a long time of waiting.

After a long time of not wanting.

After a long time of resisting.

After a long time of quietude.

After a long time of winter sleep.

After a long time of silence.

(The First Voice thinks about saying "my silence has always been a great scream" but he doesn't say it. Or maybe he is saying it. But the Second Voice doesn't hear him. Or maybe he is not listening.)

He (Second Voice) continues.

After a long *I don't want to endure anymore.*

After a long *what kind of a world this is.*

After a long life, a long death, a long stay, a long long ruin, a long long after an after:

Such a long walk it was, says the First Voice.

Such a long crawling, corrects the Second Voice.

Up to here, we came, says the First Voice.

You always say the same things, says the Second Voice.

I've always said the same things, says the First Voice. You're right. But my departure points have been different.

Nolens volens, says the Second Voice.

Please, says the First Voice. Always willingly.

Willingly or not, what does it matter? says the Second Voice. What matters is this winter we experience. As if it'll never end. Snow will melt. The day will come, surely it'll melt. Patience. I know that. I always said. Night ends. Day rises. If I said it, I meant to say it this way; this is how I thought. I looked at the summit covered by the glacier & thought: The snow will melt; the day will come and it will melt. Patience.

While being patient, says the First Voice, talk, say something, something as a coin of the realm. Propose an action.

TO GO OUT! shouts the Second Voice.

Why are you waiting? says the First Voice.

I will go out, says the Second Voice.

In this nighttime? says the First Voice.

In this nighttime, says the Second Voice.

Let's go out then, says the First Voice.

Come on, says the Second Voice.

Come on, says the First Voice.

They pretend like going out to the
Snowy,
Cold,
Frightening, with the dogs barking,
Moonless,
Dark night.

Where are you? says the Second Voice.
Silence.
Where are you? says the Second Voice.
Silence.
No answer.

Buried under the snow? Got frozen right after going out? Lost your way? (The Second Voice talks by himself in the night frost.) Where are you? He calls out again.

You give the answer, a voice comes from afar. (This is the First Voice.)

An easy answer, says the Second Voice.

Give the easy answer, says the First Voice. I'm listening to you.

Here, in a corner of our room on this mountaintop, says the Second Voice. We're shrinking, entering into ourselves, talking to ourselves, asking questions to ourselves, giving answers to ourselves, pouring out our grief to ourselves, making love to ourselves.

Haven't we gone out yet? says the First Voice. Haven't we reached others yet? Haven't the others entered into our loneliness?

Our loneliness is always plural, says the Second Voice.

Where are the peoples of this plurality? Here? Where? says the First Voice.

Them... They are there... stutters the Second Voice. Outside. Inside. Gathered in a room. Around the floor furnace. Kids and all. Women, girls, boys. Some crouched in a corner, lay down. Tomorrow morning they'll get up. Tomorrow morning they'll get up; some of them will go to the sheepfold, will take the sheep out. Some will climb the hill and will bring some grass with the sledges. If someone dies tonight, some will bury him at daybreak. (I advised them to dig deeper graves and to keep the graves away from the river.) Some will knead dough; will roll flat bread. Some will cook some cracked wheat soup. (Maybe they'll bring a bowl of it to you), some will come to school. Will talk to you. Will teach you a word. Will learn a word from you. Pour their grief to you. Have a conversation with you.

Now, at this moment, where are they? says the First Voice.

There, beyond the snow, under their soil roofs, says the Second Voice. They must be sleeping.

Are they sleeping? says the First Voice.

As always, says the Second Voice.

I don't know about that, maybe you're mistaken, says the First Voice.

About what? says the Second Voice.

Maybe they're thinking, I meant, says the First Voice.

About what? says the Second Voice.

Who knows? says the First Voice. Maybe about nothing. Maybe about everything. Maybe about yesterday. Maybe about today. Maybe about tomorrow. Maybe about all at the same time.

Or about the endless winter. About the spring, close at hand. About their wives. About their husbands. About their children. About their sheep. About the flat bread in their stomachs. About the work to do and food to make tomorrow. About the breasts they caress (or will caress). About the lips they'll kiss (or kissed). About the necks they'll bite. About the brides they'll make scream. Who knows, maybe some of them, about you.

Do you suppose? says the Second Voice.

Looking from outside, they have no worries, you'd say. They only live, you'd say. Inside their heads is too confusing; you don't see if they think or not. You doubt if their eyes see or not, their ears hear or not. You wouldn't understand if they hear, if they understand or not, as long as you look from outside.

They're like us, says the Second Voice. Are you saying this?

When you enter in, says the First Voice.

Let's enter in them then, says the Second Voice.

Not before time, says the First Voice.

It's never late, says the Second Voice.

This time let's go out for real, this time let's go to them for real, this time let's tell them for real, says the First Voice.

Corrects the Second Voice:

Let's understand them.

Let's tell about them.

No later than tomorrow, says the First Voice.

It's already tomorrow, says the Second Voice.

(One night:

Do you know, says the First Voice, lately you talk like you're investigating?

I'm probably investigating myself, answers the Second Voice.

Is this political sadism? asks the First Voice.

No, no dice, says the Second Voice. Mine is only lining up the questions without an answer. Before the mirror. Without torture.

But isn't this torture, too? says the First Voice.

This is torture, too, says the Second Voice.

(One syllable:

Is —

(One morning:

I saw a dream tonight, says the First Voice.

Hope it was good, says the Second Voice.

In my dream I saw that I was not a teacher but a student and put on trial, says the First Voice.

Dreams are the backside of facts, you know, says the Second Voice. It seems they'll be the front side for you. If you ask for a dream interpretation, according to the knowledge I inherited from my father, I would say: With the help of god, you will soon ride out the storm.

(One noon:

What're we going to eat? says the First Voice.
A big feast, says the Second Voice. Flat bread. Heart and brain, skewered. Molded cheese on top of that. To prevent him from licking his lips, he adds: Of course what we'll eat is only the first & the last ones.

(One afternoon:

Why did these dogs you fed bite you? says the First Voice.
They should have some human blood inside their veins, says the Second Voice, instead of some wolf blood.

(One evening:

How horrifying the sunset is here, says the First Voice.
But it rises beautifully, says the Second Voice.

(One daybreak:

Do you hear, over the melting snow,
the rotten bones
& the first grasses turning green
The night the wind blows.
Do you hear (always the Second Voice speaking), with each prugger till, I mean trigger pull.

My heart bleeds.

ENOUGH! shouts the First Voice. Don't tell about your life.

But at daybreak the girls become very beautiful here, says the Second Voice. Let me tell.

First, it's not daybreak right now, says the First Voice. Second, there're no women, girls around us. Third…

Yes, third? — says the Second Voice.

Third is, you began talking like a third voice. Fall silent.

He (a stranger) salls filent.

Part II

And close to spring
A winter night
Snow melts
When the sunlight
Reflects on
The perennials
When your mirror is broken
Coming across the others
And getting to know them —

How did we end up here? says the Second Voice.

In two stops, says the First Voice. You will remoment, the first stop was a town by a lake. We got there by plane. After a five-and-a-half-hour trip. It was a summer day. Down below the plane, under the sunlight, the lake was like a fairy tale, shining like an unbelievably huge emerald. You landed at the dusty and hot airport. Then in a shabby bus, jerkily, passing the outskirts and a straight road with poplar trees, you reached the town center.

When you got off the bus, a man took your luggage. Without asking you. He was skinny, tall, old, with a bushy mustache. He led the way. You didn't open your mouth and ask anything. ("He must know something.") You followed him all the way to the hotel. You stayed by yourself in a room for two. Your second arrival was by train. After traveling for two days and two nights, you reached the other side of the river. Night had already fallen. (Night falls early here, now you know.) In your hand was your old leather luggage, which had been your companion on many journeys. You crossed the lake, at midnight, during a horrible frost (winter was close at hand). There were soldiers by you, sleeping, snoring; awake, singing a folk song.

When you reached the town, it was pitch dark. They had told you beforehand, you knew. "After midnight a power outage happens in this town. You won't be able to even find this much light in the town you go to." But even in that darkness you found a phaeton. Your teeth were chattering because of the cold. Again, you didn't open your mouth and say anything to the coachman. He dropped you off at the same hotel, which the skinny, tall, old, bushy mustached one that carried your luggage on your first trip brought you to. Not even a word came out of your mouth. Neither yours, nor his. He put the money you gave him into his pocket without even looking at it, and disappeared in the darkness of the night. There was no room at this hotel. At none of the hotels in this town. I want a room for one, you said. The hotelkeeper stared at you oddly and told you that there are no rooms for one at the hotels in that town. Make it a room for two then, I'll pay for two beds, you said. We have an available bed but not an available room, he said. I can't stay in the same room with strangers, you said. No problem, you'll get used to it, he said. Nolens volens, you were to spend the night in a room where a stranger snores. (Later on, you stayed in rooms with many people snoring. And slept well. You even saw beautiful dreams.) That night, you tossed and turned, couldn't sleep well. A pillow, discolored because of dirt. An unlit light bulb, hanging from the ceiling. A gas lamp, on the bedside. The adventure begins, you thought. I suppose, that was during your first trip.

You woke up early in the morning and went out to wander around town. You had to continue the trip. You looked for a vehicle that would go to the town you were to go to. There is a bus that will depart. But what time it will depart, who knows. The bus needs to be full. When would it be full? Uncertain. Stop by on each hour. Don't worry, we'll wait. We wouldn't leave without you.

For your breakfast, you entered a milk shop. Milk, butter, honey. Then you walked all the way to Hükumet Square, and got back. You stopped by the office. Not full yet. There are only ten passengers. You went out to wander around town. Side streets. Adobe houses. Earth roads. Graveyard. Such a weird graveyard that was. Decorated with crooked pieces of rock. Yes, all these things were during your first trip. On your second trip you got to know the town much better. (Because, you waited for three days for a vehicle to depart. If the jeep of the highway authorities didn't arrive, you would've waited way longer.)

Do you know this town? This old town? This weird town?

I don't know. But you wandered around every inch of it. You went up to its castle. You went down to its lake. I don't know why, you observed and took pictures of the aqueducts and pipes constructed thousands of years ago. If I'm not mistaken, you also got into the lake. (Or maybe this was during your first trip?) You went to the small island on the lake, and rented a motorboat to see the ruins of the church. You climbed steep rocks to see this church.

It can be said that this was a touristic journey — if the rest didn't happen.

Yes, says the Second Voice, listening with patience, up until that moment. I remoment all. But there is something I don't understand: Why are you saying "You"? You were there, too, by me, like now.

Yes, says the First Voice. Right. I was there, too.

So? says the Second Voice.

Not to say, I, says the First Voice.

I understand, says the Second Voice. Continue.

If you continue to screw up the talk like this, I can't continue to anything, says the First Voice.

The talk should be interrupted every now & then in my opinion. Disrupt, dismember, disperse.

Right, says the First Voice. To not to lose ourselves too much in our voice, our exuberance, our memories, our moments.

Especially, in the flow of time, says the Second Voice.

Time, meaning the events that surround us, says the First Voice.

Also to resist the drift of words, says the Second Voice.

To stay all by ourselves, says the First Voice.

To the best of our ability, says the Second Voice.

To protect our integrity, says the First Voice.

To the best of our ability, says the Second Voice.

And our reality, says the First Voice.

They remain silent. Then:

Will you continue? says the Second Voice.

I wish, says the First Voice. But each time, you disorient me. You cause difficulties. You interrupt my talk. You prevent my success.

No problem, says the Second Voice. You always walk like this. Always in the dark & on rough terrain.

Right, says the First Voice. Like blind, even during the day. Always groping. Yet still, we got pretty far out. If we've ever accomplished anything, this is it.

If this could be called an accomplishment, says the Second Voice.

Don't you believe in this being an accomplishment? says the First Voice. Under these conditions. With these resources. By the fact that we're here now, at this moment, we came all the way up to here, and we can still continue?

This must be an accomplishment, says the Second Voice. In our own right, of course.

Of course, says the First Voice.

How befuddled you were looking around during your first trip, says the First Voice. You went to the marketplace of the town. The marketplace meant people to you. Locks and mortise forged by hammer smiths were being sold there. Ewers and vessels in the coppersmiths. Then stoves converted from gas barrels. Wheat, flour, felt, rugs, canvas, rock salt, dry apricots, comb honey, empty sacks, babies made of plastic, and old people's shoes (in this climate, especially during the upcoming winter months, I don't know how they wear these?), rifles, guns, bullets, cartridges, pocketknives, grindstones, black and red pepper, some plant roots, herbed cheese, yogurt in bowls, cotton beds, comforters, pillows, blankets, & all kinds of purveyances, which I cannot remoment now, or I forgot. The first thing you bought was a pocketknife. Three headed, its haft was made of deer antler. All of the three heads were blunt. You found a grinder and had it sharpened.

Yes, the marketplace meant people to you. With a poşu around their heads, a potur around their legs, black vests around their backs, with their suntanned faces people were looking at you. Some were approaching, saying something, in a language you didn't understand. (Now you understand it in the least. At least while asking for water: "Abı mine" you learned to say. And to say the sun, to say the dog, to say the child. To say sick, to say winter, village, town, death. In their language.) You liked the town's graveyard a lot. Crooked stones. Pieces of rock. There were no words written, no marble tombs. You took countless pictures here, too. We'll see what comes out when you develop them.

At last, you joined the bus that gathered its passengers. You took your luggage from the hotel, and by that bus, who knows what model Desoto, you hit the road, thirty-three people — counting the driver and the driver's attendant. By you, someone whose gun was visible. A 30 to 40 years old, short, blonde, pudgy man. He started the conversation. After quite some time (when his questions finished) you asked: Are you a police officer? No, a soldier. He had been in service as the gendarme commander for a year, in the furthest district of the town you were to go to. He was also the governor of the district. You were befuddled. How come? He explained: Whoever arrives doesn't stay. They quit and leave. We're soldiers. We can't do such a thing. Eh, since it's not possible without a district governor, we do that, too. He was returning from his annual leave, this gendarme commander / district governor. His wife & kids were in the capital city. During the second week after he had arrived in the district, the wife of the judge in the district had died while giving birth. Because this had daunted him, he had never brought his wife & kids. Also, the kids were going to the school. He needed to endure this separation for one year. Duty was duty. This was out of his hands. Only in winter, after December, it was a little hard. There were times he hadn't been able to hear from his family, for months. The road that connects the district to the town had been closed for at least four months. These were the first impressions of the town you were heading to. The bus driver gave a break for lunch, at the foot of a high castle, by a stream. The autumn sun was scorching all around. You sat at a table with the gendarme commander / district governor. He ordered stuffed peppers with meat. You asked for some herbed cheese & some grapes. Hard. Sour. Mountain grapes that only mature toward autumn.

When you reached the town, it was evening.

Can we call this a town?

Of course it has a governor.

Then there is a gathering place.

Then there is an inn — as all the Anatolian inns, Palas was added to the end of its name.

It also has a marketplace: two soup kitchens, three grocery-purveyance stores, a hammer smith, a lawyer-scrivener, a clothing store, a Sümer Bank, two coffee houses, a Ziraat Bank.

Mountains surrounding all four sides. Rocky cliffs. No trees. Stupendous. Especially during the nights without the moon, frightening.

Houses? A few hundred adobe houses. Scattered. I looked at the people I came across on the roads. As if I saw the Human for the first time. Legs with potur. Defeated gazes. Wrapped heads. Droopy mustaches. They looked back at me, too. As if they saw a Human for the first time.

With my luggage in my hand, I went to Sümbül Palas.

There was a bed, *for me*. In a room with five beds, an empty bed. As if reserved for me.

I put my luggage under the bed. Just when I went out to look for a place to eat my fill, a young man that looked like me (who isn't from here) approached.

Welcome.

Came well.

We knew you were coming. We were waiting for you. Please, let's go to the gathering place.

We went to the gathering place. A place packed with military officers. I ordered eggs with soudjouk. Also a bottle of rakı. A few reserve officers gathered around us. The one who brought me there introduced me. They were all staring at my face with pity.

They exiled you here?

And you?

I poured my rakı to my glass. The glasses of the ones around me were lifted. In honor of my new exile.

Someone said, In here we drink alone. This is the country of the exiled. Then patted my shoulder. Never mind, one gets used to it. I told him that I don't mind & I won't get used to it. He was befuddled. How will you live then? How will you endure for two years?

Mankind endures, I said.

We will see, he said.

We saw, you see.

Did I get used to it?
Didn't you get used to it?

During that trip, you stayed for four days in this town, all in all. You fell sick on the fourth day.

The only doctor of this town said, you need to be hospitalized; in here, as you see, there is noone except this caregiver & me. Let me send you to the neighboring town that has a hospital.

You put the transfer paper into your pocket and jumped on the first bus. You went to the neighboring town, to the State Hospital in the neighboring town. They looked at people as if they were looking at dogs, in here. The doctor who was to see you didn't understand the problems of the people whose language he didn't understand. Because you were talking in his language, or because your clothes looked alike, he paid more attention to you than the others.

And he said, we don't have the machines in here to make the necessary screenings. Let's send you to the town that has a "fully equipped" hospital.

You waited for the plane departing in two days.

You landed in the town that had a "fully equipped" hospital. Surrounded with ramparts, with its narrow alleys, it was a hot and beautiful medieval town.

The following day (you fell in love such that) you forgot your sickness, neglected the hospital, and went out to wander around town.

You spent a few hours in its marketplace.

You watched the coppersmiths and hammer smiths.

You watched the villagers who were exchanging flour for cotton, cotton for copper pots & pans, tea, cheese, & sugar.

You looked at the women with their dangling silver nose rings, tall, brunette, walking upright, staring straight into one's eyes, jamming money between their breasts. At the young girls selling bowls of yogurt. Then, you went to the museum near the marketplace. (An old habit.) Among the stones in the museum, one of them especially attracted your interest. A tombstone of a French child who was born in this town, died in this town, was buried in this town (you don't know even today why that was put into a museum).

Birth date: 1865

Death date: 1872

If I'm not mistaken.

Then you got on a phaeton (before noon), didn't open your mouth and say a thing to the coachman.

To the brothels.

He took you to the outskirts of the town.

With humane prostitutes

beautiful houses

hot, clean rooms

where customers were offered silk pajamas

& hot, well-steeped teas.

Do you remoment our return? says the Second Voice.

Return from the brothel? says the First Voice.

We know that, says the Second Voice. Return to the town we came from.

How could I not remoment? says the First Voice. Same roads. Same dust. Same smoke. But this time there was no sense of suffocation in your heart. As if this round trip made a man of you. Educated you. Made you get used to it (almost).

Again in the evening we reached the town. The town without lights. Again we ate dinner at the gathering place; again we stayed (six people in one room) at that place (Sümbül Palace), snoring, coughing, along with sweat & foot odor.

Next day, they told you which village you needed to go to, the Second Voice takes the words out of his mouth. You had no idea about this place. Neither did the people who told you that you needed to go there (none of them had ever been to that place). The locals gave some unclear information. The information you had before you hit the road was that it was a very high village. And after a seventy-two kilometers bus ride, for five hours you needed to climb the mountain on a horse or a mule.

You thought it was funny. You were to get on a horse for the first time. You waited for a bus the next morning, but couldn't find one. You wanted to go as soon as possible. A truck driver that brought purveyance to the village told you: "Come if you can travel in the back." (The seat by him was held for a military officer.) In the back, with you, a father and a son were traveling.

Don't tell, says the First Voice. This is not the right time. Don't tell. I'm getting goose bumps.

Why? says the Second Voice. Why? You probably found this short trip interesting, too, such that, once you reached the village (or later) you wrote about it in your diary. Since you don't want, I won't tell. I'll read your note.

And from the notebook before him, he opens a book-marked page and starts reading:

14 November

We were traveling in the back of a truck. Me and a father and son next to me. Bags and sacks beside them. They must have come to get some provisions, I thought. Just after we hit the road I tried to talk to them. The child didn't understand my language and glared at me. His father gave me some in-formation about the area with the Turkish he learned during military training. From time to time I couldn't help looking at the sack the child was sitting on. On the sacks was written UNICEF. The openings of the sacks were sealed. I asked out of curiosity: What's in them? Where are they coming from? Who are they giving these to? How much? Why?

The father said, these are donations for us. At times we go to town to get these donations.

Do they give these to everyone? I said.

No, only to lepers, he said.

Are you a leper? I said.

He thrust his hands toward me and in his language, told his son to thrust his out, too. (The son didn't comply with this request.)

Yes, he said. Both my son & I are lepers. So are my wife & other children.

Can you tell about the way you got to the village?

I got off the truck in front of a gendarmerie station, says the First Voice. I had a bag made of American fabric, in which I put food, drinks, and clothes. I put the bag on my back and entered the station. I told the gendarme my duty and the village I was to go to. (They looked at my face with pity, too.) I wanted them to accompany me or to find me a guide. Of course, I would pay for the horse ride for myself and my guide, along with his fee.

The gendarmes, in one voice, told me that the commander was not in the station and before he comes back, they wouldn't be able to go; and explained that to find a horse (or a mule) was as hard as finding a guide. In the meantime they poured a glass of tea, which was brewing on top of the burning stove. While drinking our teas, we talked about the lives they live, about the winter, about their homelands. One of them was coming from a Black Sea village, his father died last winter, but because the roads were closed he couldn't attend his father's funeral, he was burning up about that. Another one was from a western city; he had olive groves, a wife, and two children. Yet another one was from Thrace. He said, we are kind of fellow townsmen. He was a young boy, blonde & stutter-ing, with a beard just springing out. Yet another one was lying in the bed, sleeping (you were told that he was always sleeping like that).

We were drinking our teas.

By our fifth or seventh glass, with two gendarmes near him, the commander (sustained sergeant) came. We greeted one another. The gendarmes told him about the situation. The commander assigned two gendarmes. They wouldn't be able to come with me all the way to the village I was to go to; but they would be able to accompany me up until the first village on the way and from that village they might be able to find a villager along with a horse (or a mule). There were dogs, first of all. Second, the villag-ers might get scared of the gendarmes and comply with renting me a horse (or a mule) at least. It wouldn't be easy acquiring that by myself. The gendarmes who would ac-company me girded on their cartridges, took their rifles. I put my bag on my back & we hit the road. We climbed up a steep hill. I was out of breath at the end of the hill. One of the gendarmes said, the village you're to go to is the highest one of the region. Once it snows, there's no way for you to come down again.

I have no intention to anyway, I said.

After the steep hill, we began proceeding in a flat, but muddy path. There was no village in sight. Only bare mountains and trees that shed their leaves. And some weird birds flying by.

NOONE

So long after, I saw the village. First the school, then the houses. When approaching the village, dogs surrounded us. The gendarmes scared them with the rifles and we proceeded. When we reached in front of a two-story house, with the barking of the dogs, some people came out and invited us in. We went in. We rested for a while, drinking tea. We spoke of the situation to the owner of the house and the other villagers who swarmed into the room. We told them where I was to go.

I want to rent a horse (or a mule) & if possible a guide.

The owner of the house said, there is noone in the village now. Because there is noone, there is no horse (or mule) either.

The gendarmes insisted.

Then he said he would give his own horse (but only up to the neighboring village).

There was nothing to do. I took his horse. His son (a thirteen to fourteen years old kid), who brought the horse, led the way. The gendarmes and I said farewell to each other. We hit the path; they went down toward their station and I went up toward my village. I was getting on a horse for the first time since I was a kid. A horse without a saddle, stirrup. Thank god it was not a grumpy horse. We proceeded following the goat path. At a distance, we spotted a village with four to five — the roofs were almost level with the ground — adobe houses. The child leading the way turned his head. Na, Evranis, he said. This must have been the name of the village: Evranis.

128

Neither the names, the villages, the mountains, nor the locals were making me befuddled any longer. As if I was returning to my hometown, which I left years ago, where I was born and raised. And (as if) I was embarrassed of myself for forgetting how to ride a horse and forgetting these paths and this language.

We got to the village. And the child in front stopped before a dunghill.

I jumped off the horse.

After jumping off the horse, continues the Second Voice, we greeted the ones gathered in front of the house. The child that brought us here told them who we were, where we were going, what we wanted, I suppose. A skinny man held our hand and took us in. It smelt like soot and was dark. A room without windows. Only an air hole in the ceiling. There, in that faint light (when I went in they lit an oil lamp) I saw a child wrapped in rags. He was fighting for his life. I asked what was wrong with him. In my language. They understood what I said. They removed the rags. I came across a naked child, burnt all the way up to his neck. He is dying. Almost dead. I asked why they didn't take him to town, to the health center in town. The child who brought me here translated the things I said into their language. That skinny man (he must have been the dying child's father) lifted his shoulders; said some things at length. I understood only the word Allah. I went out, opened my bag, & amongst the medicines I found a burn ointment. I gave it. I told them to apply it to the entire body. Knowing that it would not do a thing.

The child who brought me here was holding the horse mane, growing impatient to return in no time. To him, I asked if he could or couldn't find a horse (or a mule) for me, to rent. He talked to the skinny man I gave the medicine to. When I heard a sharp Na sound coming out of him, I put the bag on my shoulder and to the child I asked which path I should follow to get to the village. He showed me a narrow path that was winding around the lake. If I were to follow this path I'd reach my village. I greeted noone. I said goodbye to noone. I hit the path.

It was fifteen to twenty minutes after I got out of the village; I came across a villager preceding a few sheep. Coming after him, a horse whose bridle he was holding. I quickened my steps, reached over & greeted him.

Selamunaleykum.

Aleykumselam.

I told him who I was, the village I was to go to.

Where you're to go to is too far and too high, he said. Take my horse. It will take you all the way up to our village. You can stay in our place tonight. We can go to the village together tomorrow morning.

I didn't want to take his horse and told him that we could walk together.

The path is long and steep, take the horse, he said.

I jumped on the horse. It was a gray horse. I put my bag in front of me.

All right, I said, and hit the path.

Admit that you got scared in the beginning, says the Second Voice.

I did, says the First Voice. I didn't know the way. And all four sides were mountains and stones. I did what the villager who gave me the horse told me to; I held the bridle loosely: "The horse knows the way."

He was jumping over the stones with slow, cautious steps. And it was moving forward without being startled, as if knowing that the rider on its back was a stranger (moreover a novice). If I'm not mistaken we went on like this for almost two hours. All along the way not coming across one single living being (neither human, nor animal). At last, at a distance, a few houses appeared in sight. The sun had almost set. We passed a river. Then we reached the village. The horse didn't stop there. Maybe, its place is not here, I thought. Regardless of the barks and attacks of the dogs, it stopped in front of one of the houses at the far end of the village, my gray horse. Some women came out of the house. They began shouting in one voice and bombarded me with questions. I didn't know how to respond. Some were crying. At last a man from the village who knows my language came by. And to him I said that nothing happened to the owner of the horse, that he gave me his horse, that he would reach the village with the sheep soon enough. They took the horse. They took my bag. They invited me in. The pillows were set. Sheepskins were laid out. The stove was burning. Tea was brewed. After a long while, the villager who gave me his horse (his name was Hasso, I learned this that night) came with the sheep.

I spent that night in Hasso's house. The next morning, right after sunrise, we hit the path. He was in front, I was behind. Two horsemen.

Can you tell us how you got to the village, how you were greeted, and your first impressions?

I got tired, says the First Voice. Some other time.

I will tell, says the Second Voice. Because I was also there. That was me on one of the two horses. Now, I will tell. And I will tell *objectively*. He can remain silent, if he wants, may he never speak again.

At first, monstrous dogs welcomed us
in Pirkanis (our village!).

Thank god we had a horse.

And thank god Hasso was in front of us.

The village was set on a hillside (the furthest end, the highest hill of the region).

We glimpsed around, not counting the sheepfolds & the school.

There were thirteen houses.

Thirteen adobe houses. We counted.

The population (including women and children), we learned later: A hundred-and-fourteen people.

We left the horses by the fountain.

We walked to the biggest house of the village, behind the fountain.

Some people — who came out of their houses because of the barking dogs — looked at us.

Hasso, before entering that big house, answered the questions of the ones who surrounded us.

We entered the house.

We took off our shoes.

They took us in a room.

A large, bright room with high ceilings.

Earth floor, grass roof.
At first, someone bulky entered the room.
Shook our hands.
We learned about his identity: The headman. His name was Mustafa.
Then the others entered.
Fifteen to twenty men.
Most of them didn't know Turkish.
I was talking, headman or Hasso was translating.
The headman's first question was this:
Are you permanent here?
I am permanent.
For real?
For real.

The Second Voice hesitates here.
You were to speak objectively, says the First Voice.
I will continue, says the Second Voice.
The stove was burning.
A while later, a tea-urn was brought.
The ones filling the room, crouching by the walls, were eying me from head to toe.
Hands on the knees.
Then on a copper tray the tea glasses were brought.
In a cup, broken into tiny pieces, the sugar cubes. The hands on the knees reached for the glasses. A child, whose mustache was just springing out, standing, hand and foot, filled the glasses with the tea,

the first glass was given to me
then to Hasso
then to the headman
then to the others
Meanwhile a girl brought some herbed cheese on a plate
and some flat bread
she put them in front of me
I put a piece of cheese on the flat bread & wrapped it;
I had a sip of my tea,
drinking their tea, they were staring at me
how do I eat
how do I drink the tea
my glass was always full
the young boy whose mustache was just springing out
was refreshing it
at some point the door opened
a girl
by her
a boy two to three years old, with scissor-trimmed hair
his nose drooling
came in
settled by the stove
On her
a patchy dirty dress
with red flowers
everyone in the room
began laughing
I didn't know

I didn't understand why
meanwhile
Through the doorway
I saw a young girl
she upon seeing that I saw
ran away, chuckling
I was sipping on my sixth glass of tea
Hasso stood
Shook the hands, first mine, then the others
They brought his horse in front of the door
He jumped on his horse
The horse I rode was behind
they left the village
In front of the door, I waved
I returned to the room
Headman Mustafa
one more time, asked my name
then, he asked if I understand the sick or not
I have medicine in my bag, I said
Thereupon they took me to one of the houses close by
Here too, it was dark, without a window, an air hole in
the ceiling
a room
there was no stove in here
there was a floor furnace
there was soot
there was smoke
in here too, they lit an oil lamp

under the flickering light of the oil lamp made of a Carlsberg can, which even today I still have no idea from where, how it ended up in here,

I looked at the child

They uncovered her

They were showing

A horrible swollen stomach

It was the first time I ever saw such a thing

Not only the child's (about two years old) stomach, but also her feet, hands, and face were swollen

& black & blue

Not a sickness I have known

Headman said, make an injection

To the town, take her to the doctor, I said

I was afraid of making an injection

Because she was dying

because she was about to die

I asked the young man by her side. Are you her father?

Headman translated my question into his language & he answered.

Her mother is there (in the dark, crouching by one of the walls, young or old I cannot tell), her father isn't in the village, her father is far away, and this is her uncle.

There is nothing that can be done, may god save her.

The Second Voice remains silent.

And god didn't save her, right? says the First Voice.

Yes, says the Second Voice. You asked about the child once you woke up. Headman said that she died at midnight and was buried in the morning. You saw a mark of pain in noone's face.

You wrote down in your notebook, death is natural here, says the First Voice.

Yes, says the Second Voice. A few days later, when her father came & learned about his child's death, he took it so naturally. He stopped by your place that day, & talked to you as if nothing happened.

Halit, says the First Voice.

Yes, says the Second Voice. He returned from a long trip.

Halit, says the First Voice.

Yes, says the Second Voice. Halit, whose story I will tell, even if not here, even if not now, somewhere else, one day.

Yes, says the First Voice. Certainly.

Then, says the Second Voice. Why not now?

Now is not the time, says the First Voice.

Why not? says the Second Voice.

Maybe it will never be the time.

Right, says the First Voice.

You can begin with the first day he stopped by your place, says the Second Voice.

Let's begin with that, says the First Voice.

It was a week after his child's death.
I moved out of headman's house & settled in my lodge.

I set up my stove converted from a gas barrel; I made my mattress with my own hands.

It was evening when my door was opened & he came in. He greeted me, sat across. He told me who he was. I gave my sympathies when I learned who he was. Sympathy for all, he said. He remained silent. With a need to say something, there was nothing that can be done, I said. Who knows, he said; if I were here, maybe she wouldn't have died. Where were you? I asked. Somewhere far away, he said.

I was looking at this slim, short man, sitting across from me on his heels, rolling his cigarette with the tobacco he took from his pocket. He must have been around forty years old. (Later on, I learned that he was two years younger than me.)

That night he didn't stay too long.

While leaving, when I'm here, let me know if you need anything, don't ask someone else, he said.

Next morning, I asked the headman about him. That morning he got away.

Days, weeks passed; he didn't return.

I was seeing only his wife and children in the village.

In the meantime, I collected some information from the villagers about him. Information that didn't match up.

Headman was saying: Halit is the brother of my second wife, Zazi. They are actually from Yuksekova. He became an orphan when he was a baby; they grew up with our landlord. Our landlord's mother breast-fed Halit. Once I married Zazi and once Halit's business broke apart, he migrated here with his wife and children. I gave him that place you saw in the village. He built a house. He doesn't have land. He smuggles. Brings goods and sells them. He can't take fieldwork, grass work. If he asks for money, don't give. You can't get it back.

Hasan (headman's younger brother): Watch out for Halit, man, he doesn't have right or wrong. He can even stab his own brother; he has no religion or faith. No pity. He killed two people. One of them was Acem. He was put in jail. Our landlord rescued him.

Süleyman's statement: Halit, I don't know, a good kid. He's weird. He's unlike us. He doesn't have land. He doesn't have animals, except one or two chickens. He got a girl last winter. He brought her here, locked her in the house. He left the village after fifteen days. He hasn't returned for three months. Meanwhile, the girl's father came, got the girl back, and left. Halit is in love with this girl. He will ambush and shoot the girl's father tomorrow if not today. You can't find a better sniper than Halit in this region.

Headman Landlord (headman's seventy-years-old fa-ther): These are kids, they can't handle two women, even one is too much for them. I have three wives, and I would overpower all three of them. This is Kerem, my son. Eight years old. This is my third wife, here.

Seyit: Halit is good. I haven't heard a bad word from him. He drinks, but what's it to us? He's a brave guy. For three years he messed with noone, stole noone's goods, touched noone's daughter, played with noone's flock. A brave guy he is, Halit.

Alone in the room

In the room alone
In the room I'm alone
By myself

He's not talking to himself tonight
He's cold
He trembles
He threw in the last two pieces of dung just a little
while ago
Suddenly warmed the stove
The stove warmed the room
Now the warmth is fading away
His teeth are chattering
His lips turn purple
His eyes fixated somewhere on the wall
He doesn't try to warm himself
He doesn't want to get in the bed (as if)
He is not talking, yes
And not thinking
Sitting on his mattress cross-legged staring at the
books and papers on the bedside as if staring at a living
being

He takes a book Opens He quits without reading

He takes an envelope Opens He tears up the letter and throws it away before getting to the end

He opens the lid of the stove & throws the letter on top of the fading ashes

Again he returns to his mattress

Again he sits cross-legged

Again his eyes are fixed to a spot on the wall

No

His lips are black and blue

Black and blue lips (only) tremble

His teeth are chattering

Dogs are again howling outside

A stranger is approaching

Or the wolves are coming down again

With no period no comma no question with no ending dead night goes on like this in fragments

Goes on in fragments

Night

Dead

With no ending

No question

No period

No comma

No exclamation

No ending dead night like this in fragments goes on
with no period no comma no question no exclamation

Alone in the room
In the room alone
He too is alone

He gets up from the couch where he was laying.

I made this mattress. On the fifth day of my arrival. I took the remaining wood from the construction site of the school. I took a hammer, a saw, and a few nails from the carpenter of the village — what was his name, Aladdin's father? — I cut. I sawed. I put the wood aside. I made a wooden couch thirty centimeters high from the floor. Headman gave me a cotton mattress. I laid this mattress over the couch.

I brought two bed sheets with me here.

Two embroidered pillow covers.

I didn't have a comforter.

I had a blanket.

I laid the blanket over the mattress. The rug over the blanket. My cloak (at nights) over the rug.

The coach is right in the corner.

The wind coming in through the bottom of the door roams around my feet at nights.

My feet are under these three layers; blanket–rug–cloak. Don't feel the cold night wind. As for my bedside, the wall is covered with felt in here. The felt that Ramazan beat with the children at school. I asked Ramazan for a pattern to be put on this felt. He said, he ain't know. Although I drew one and gave it to him, he didn't put it on.

(He beat this felt with ten okka of cotton he got for 7.50 liras per kilogram. He charged me an additional 30 liras for his labor.)

I undress to have dinner in the evenings when there is wood in the stove. I untie the cotton belt around my waist and retie it. I throw my cloak over the bed. I wear my pajamas. I put on the headpiece my mother knitted, the one I wear while fishing, in the past, and I pull it all the way down to my neck. Such that only my mouth, my nose, and my eyes remain uncovered. I get in my bed like this, not to get frozen.

He opens the window shutters.

It's still nighttime.

The moon reflects on the snow.

He looks at the grand mountains illuminated by the moonlight. In the distance, a few trees burst out of the snow. Only the branches, dry, weak branches, are visible, and their shadows reflect on the snow. His eyes seek a path over the snow. There are none. Snow covers them. The snow, still falling. Flaky. But unlike the snow in the evening. It quite slowed down. Such that, he can see the moonlight reflecting on the snow, and the hills across are illuminated by that. There is no frost. Weird, kind of mild weather. Even the dogs aren't barking. Silence.

He had his cloak on. And his cotton headpiece. He unbuttoned his pajamas. He didn't light the lamp. The moon illuminates the window area along with other parts of the room, as outside. The light outside is like the light before sunrise. Comforting. Restful. However, it's not even two at night or two in the morning.

He takes the can by the wall right across from the window. An uncovered, empty can. The brand is readable: TAMEK.

He holds it close by and pisses in it. Steam comes out. After he's done pissing, he approaches the window again with the can. He opens the window & pours the can over the snow. Then he fills the can with the snow accumulated in front of the window. He looks outside once more. He takes a deep breath. He closes the window. He closes the shutters. The room is dark. He throws the cloak over the bed. We need to try sleeping. For one or two more hours.

The sun is about to rise.

It was during the second week of your arrival, the Second Voice begins the sentence. One evening the headman came to your room. After talking about here and there, this and that, he brought up the woman issue. Headman had three wives. He got the third one on the fourth or fifth day of your arrival. He asked you

You're young

How will you live here

Here, on this mountaintop

Without women?

I'm used to it, you said.

How come you're used to it?

He stared at you, befuddled.

You're coming from the city.

You're young. How can you be used to it?

You're right. But there's nothing I can do, you said.

After a momentary hesitation, looking at you in the eyes, he asked if you were married or not.

I'm married, you said.

According to this answer, he suggested this to you:

We need to find you a girl. A girl around the age of marriage. From this village or from a neighboring village.

How much is needed? you asked.

She can be found for four to five thousand. You'd get her for cheap. Because they'd know that you wouldn't take the girl with you when leaving.

But I'm married, you said (again).

So what, said headman. We can do an imam marriage here. Because you wouldn't take the girl with you, they'd give her to you cheap. After you, her father would give her to someone else. He'd get the benefit from this deal.

After these words you thought about yourself, & also (maybe) about the girl. But still (even today I'm feeling befuddled) your answer was a certain NO.

Headman said, it's not my fault anymore, and got out of the room.

You asked yourself, Does he want to give me one of his daughters? He cares for me? Or else, He is having money issues.

After that night, days passed.

Many nights passed.

Loneliness continued in a way you weren't used to.

In the meantime (of course) the balls have swollen.

Then emptied out by themselves.

One day, they said people would come for headman's daughter, to set up a bind for a promise to wed her. Her destined marriage proposal came from a far away village of the same tribe. That day the eldest daughter of headman's, who had been bringing food to you, didn't come. When you went to headman's house before noon, you saw her washed, dressed up. He was looking at you from behind the door. You were alone in the room. A while later, she brought some tea for you. She put them in front of you, the tea and the sugar cup. Then tears falling from her eyes, she walked backwards & left.

The sound of guns and rifles burst out.

Men and women on horses entered the village.

It was sunset. You were by the fountain.

Horses stopped in front of headman's house.

Some of the people on the horses entered headman's house. Some to the headman landlord's.

The others scattered to different houses.

In the meantime a goat was cut, or a hogget.

In the evening, after the prayer, dinner was eaten. Tea was drunk. Then the other guests showed up at headman's house.

You were sitting between headman landlord and a stranger whose name you didn't know. In front of you on a large tray, cups filled with dry apricots, walnuts, & grapes were lined up.

Just a little while later, negotiations began.

Headman landlord chose İbrahim as a spokesman. He was to do the negotiation. This is the custom, they said to you. İbrahim got the floor and began praising the "goods he is to sell":

My daughter's eyes are as a gazelle's
At night they reflect light
Even at night they spot the difference between friends
& fiends.
My daughter's neck is as a dove's
Her skin is white
Her hair is silky
Her walk is joyful
She is efficient
She spins cotton
In our village she's the one who spins cotton the best

From the other side (from the groom's side), an old
man gets the floor and begins the son's praise.
Our son Yusuf
is brave
he is the apple of our village's eye
both his back and his arms are strong
he is the one
who never gives up to snow
who takes the sheep out of the sheepfold
who races the wolves up the mountains
his eyes are coal black
his horse is a steed

The mutual praises went on like this
Then the time came to discuss money
They asked headman landlord how much he wanted
for his daughter & İbrahim answered:

For your sake
since you're the brave man of our tribe
since we're from the same bloodline
since we love each other like brothers
since we wouldn't give our daughter to someone else
even for hundreds of thousands
we want ten thousand from you

The other side:
We know all about
your daughter's beauty
your daughter's dexterity
but our Yusuf doesn't have ten thousand, including his
herds.

İbrahim asked:
What does Yusuf have?
There are forty sheep his father gave to him
A hundred decare of land, which yields two-hundred
bushels of wheat a year
Two horses
One gun, one rifle
We can give fifteen of the sheep now
We can give fifty okka of cotton when the summer comes
And we can count three thousand in cash now

İbrahim:
To fifteen sheep

Fifty okka of cotton
And three thousand banknotes
No girl would come out of this village

The other side:
Three thousand and five hundred then

İbrahim:
Raise it a little

We can give six okka, and black sheep cotton

İbrahim:
If you like we can stop this business
Have our teas and go to sleep

The other side:
Two more sheep we can give.

İbrahim goes out with headman landlord and the girl's
father to talk it over. You feel weary. You sweat. You take
this opportunity and go out also. And after saying all right,
you begin walking toward your house. You have your cloak
on, and your lantern is in your hand. A smarmy dog fol-
lows you. You turn your face toward the cold. Frosting. You
get back to yourself a little. When you enter the house, you
light your gas lamp, throw a few faggots in the stove and
fire it, then put two pieces of dung on top of it. You lie on
your bed & turn on the radio.

Negotiations must be going on.

And a crushed, bruised feeling within, that weird broken feeling.

What is this
in the night
this bitterly groaning folksong?
A love song it must be
or a lamentation
or both.

What are they saying like this in one voice Harabo Harabo?

They say Harabo is bad.

Are you listening?

Yes.

What are they saying, do you understand?

A little. They are saying, come wait by my bedside.

These places I live became unlivable.

Who are they talking about you think? Who are they crying out to?

About the grapes of Aliye Ramo village.

Breasts that look like the grapes of Aliye Ramo village
Young-girl breasts

In the meantime, they hope for help from god and also from the devil

Or they give up hope from both
And they talk about a distant city

Maybe Mardin
Because they talk about a castle
Or something like that
A tower, an inn
And about a willowy girl inside it
About the body of that young girl
About her snow melting flesh
About winter nights
About spring sun
A girl such a girl
Her name is Aliye Ramo
Both a girl and a village
A folksong that talks about both a girl and a village
What else are they talking about?
About the sun that will not shine
About the cold sun
About the sheep, the hogget, the lamb yet to be born
And about the wolf coming down from the mountain
This is such a winter, such an endless winter the folk-
song says
When'll you come & find me
When'll you rescue me?
Who sings this folksong? For who was this lamenta-
tion first sung?
I don't know. I told you, either for a girl or a village, and
as you hear they're singing it in one voice now.
They say, enough is enough, Harabo, enough is enough.
What're they saying?

You married with someone else, Harabo, you betrayed me
You escaped from your village
You went to strangers
Enough is enough, Harabo
You forgot me
You forgot me
You made me a slave to yourself & you forgot me
God will not leave you unpunished
Harabo Harabo
But come back even so
Throw yourself into the arms of the one who forgives
& loves you
Harabo Harabo
You will die Harabo
Your bones will get dry; your ashes will blow in the wind
Morning wind will bring your ashes back to the land
where you were born
Will drift under the tree where we made love
Harabo Harabo my breasts are burning
Harabo Harabo my groins are scorching
Harabo the sublime mountain wind blows
Harabo this wind never stops
Until the flame within me is put out

They never remain silent.

They don't. This is an endless folksong, every time it ends
it restarts. They told me about it before I came here. It continues all night. As if they say the same things over & over again.

FERİT EDGÜ

What are they saying?
Deyola, they say, I am afraid of death.
Even if I say I'm not, I am afraid
I'm afraid of the evil eye, afraid of the sublime winter
When I'm away from you
I'm afraid of the blowing wind
From the falling snow
From the howling wolf
If I die
You come back and dig my grave
Because only you can shovel this snow & reach the earth
Because only you can dig in this sublime winter
My grave (my grave, it says)
And only you can bury me on that hill
There is no tree to plant by my side

But it's all right
The snow would melt if you were here
Then you'd find a tree and plant it
By the side of my flattened grave
Delaylo oy delaylo
A cruel one it is, the death that comes in winter
A cruel one it is, the death away from the beloved
Helo helo I'm still hungry for your lips
Couldn't caress you as much as I wished
How can I let go of your skin
This night, such an endless night
And bullet sounds are coming, delaylo delaylo

I looked through the window the snow begins
At a distance
High up
Among the snow
All alone
As if all alone
In the kindled flames
In the sooty light of the kindled flames
In darkness
I wouldn't want to die without you
I wouldn't die, I wouldn't want to delaylo delolo ...

Do they remain silent?
Yes. To start again in a little while.
Do you think they will start again?
I suppose.
How long you think it will take?
All night. All through the winter (maybe).
Why are they singing all through the night, all through
the winter, this endless folksong, this painful lamentation.
Because.
Like the way we do, you mean to say?
Maybe ...
Yes ...
No doubt ...
Exactly ...

From where did we begin the talk?
says the Second Voice.

Where did we begin the talk?
When did we begin the talk?
Why did we begin the talk?
WHY DID WE BEGIN THE TALK?
Don't shout, says the First Voice.
Repeats the Second Voice:
Why did we begin the talk?
Which talk? says the First Voice.
This talk, says the Second Voice.
This talk, says the First Voice, I don't remoment from
where we began? But before us this talk must've begun.
Who? says the Second Voice.
How who? says the First Voice. People, of course.
We continue alone. Is this what you want to say? says
the Second Voice.
This is what I want to say, says the First Voice.
As if taking revenge, says the Second Voice.
Taking revenge on what? says the First Voice.
On silence, says the Second Voice.
And maybe on many others, says the First Voice.
For example? says the Second Voice.

For example, on loneliness, says the First Voice.

What else?

Else? Maybe on time, says the First Voice.

The feeling of taking revenge, is that what makes us talk? says the Second Voice.

I didn't mean to say this, says the First Voice.

What other reason can there be? says the Second Voice.

To move forward where we are, it can also be, says the First Voice.

To move forward where we are? says the Second Voice. Where did we begin to talk?

Considering our talks, on a cold mountaintop, says the First Voice.

On the same mountaintop? says the Second Voice.

It has no significance, says the First Voice. We may have begun at the seaside.

In a desert maybe? says the Second Voice.

Possible, says the First Voice.

If so, we have ascended a lot, says (sarcastic) the Second Voice.

I suppose not, says the First Voice. Fortunately, I'm not so naïve as to believe that one can move forward by changing locations.

Ah, that's why you're talking about moving forward where we are, says the Second Voice.

Do you say we are moving forward? says (again sarcastic) the Second Voice.

I don't know, says the First Voice. We'll see in time. As much as our strength, our skills, our possibilities. Surely, we will proceed.

Why? says the Second Voice.

For what? says the First Voice.

Why? says the Second Voice. Why did we begin the talk?

You suppose it has a beginning? says the First Voice.

It must have, says the Second Voice.

Ours is more like a continuation, says the First Voice. Continuation of a talk that was begun in a desert, at a seaside, on lowland, on a mountaintop, in a village, in a town.

But at this moment, at least in here, since we get to talk (get the talk), we need to know why we continue, why we talk, says the Second Voice.

I've never asked this question, says the First Voice.

Are we talking about our loneliness? says the Second Voice.

As you see, says the First Voice.

Are we talking about this mountaintop? says the Second Voice.

We can say, says the First Voice.

Are we talking about the places we came from, the people we loved? says the Second Voice.

As much as we can, at least a little, as much as our memory permits, says the First Voice.

Or else about our exile? The howling of the dogs? Being amongst the cursed people as a cursed one?

I don't know, says the First Voice.

Then why're you talking? says the Second Voice. Then
why do you continue?
To tell the story of my journey, says the First Voice.

Then he remains silent.

— In the cold room, a complete silence.
Outside, the wind goes lull. Dogs stop their howling.
Inside, the stove & the lamp
One went out
The other, sooted—

January 1964–February 1974
Hakkari–Ankara
Paris–Istanbul

COLOPHON

NOONE

was typeset in InDesign CC.

The text & page numbers are set in *Adobe Jenson Pro*.
The scripts are set in *Ahoy Dreamer*.

Book design & typesetting: Alessandro Segalini
Cover design: Contra Mundum Press
Image: Egon Schiele, *Male Nude with Red Loincloth*, 1914

NOONE

is published by Contra Mundum Press.
Its printer has received Chain of Custody certification from:
The Forest Stewardship Council,
The Programme for the Endorsement of Forest Certification,
& The Sustainable Forestry Initiative.

Contra Mundum Press   New York · London · Melbourne

CONTRA MUNDUM PRESS

Dedicated to the value & the indispensable importance of the individual voice, to works that test the boundaries of thought & experience.

The primary aim of Contra Mundum is to publish translations of writers who in their use of form and style are *à rebours*, or who deviate significantly from more programmatic & spurious forms of experimentation. Such writing attests to the volatile nature of modernism. Our preference is for works that have not yet been translated into English, are out of print, or are poorly translated, for writers whose thinking & æsthetics are in opposition to timely or mainstream currents of thought, value systems, or moralities. We also reprint obscure and out-of-print works we consider significant but which have been forgotten, neglected, or overshadowed.

There are many works of fundamental significance to *Weltliteratur* (& *Weltkultur*) that still remain in relative oblivion, works that alter and disrupt standard circuits of thought — these warrant being encountered by the world at large. It is our aim to render them more visible.

For the complete list of forthcoming publications, please visit our website. To be added to our mailing list, send your name and email address to: info@contramundum.net

Contra Mundum Press
P.O. Box 1326
New York, NY 10276
USA

OTHER CONTRA MUNDUM PRESS TITLES

Gilgamesh

Ghérasim Luca, *Self-Shadowing Prey*

Rainer J. Hanshe, *The Abdication*

Walter Jackson Bate, *Negative Capability*

Miklós Szentkuthy, *Marginalia on Casanova*

Fernando Pessoa, *Philosophical Essays*

Elio Petri, *Writings on Cinema & Life*

Friedrich Nietzsche, *The Greek Music Drama*

Richard Foreman, *Plays with Films*

Louis-Auguste Blanqui, *Eternity by the Stars*

Miklós Szentkuthy, *Towards the One & Only Metaphor*

Josef Winkler, *When the Time Comes*

William Wordsworth, *Fragments*

Josef Winkler, *Natura Morta*

Fernando Pessoa, *The Transformation Book*

Emilio Villa, *The Selected Poetry of Emilio Villa*

Robert Kelly, *A Voice Full of Cities*

Pier Paolo Pasolini, *The Divine Mimesis*

Miklós Szentkuthy, *Prae, Vol. 1*

Federico Fellini, *Making a Film*

Robert Musil, *Thought Flights*

Sándor Tar, *Our Street*

Lorand Gaspar, *Earth Absolute*

Josef Winkler, *The Graveyard of Bitter Oranges*

Jean-Jacques Rousseau, *Narcissus*

SOME FORTHCOMING TITLES

Jean-Luc Godard, *Phrases*

Pierre Senges, *The Major Refutation*

Ahmad Shamlu, *Born Upon the Dark Spear*

About the Author

Ferit EDGÜ is one of the leading writers of contemporary Turkish literature & has been instrumental in developing "bunalım" (introspective speculative fiction). He writes poetry, fiction, and nonfiction, as well as essays on art & literature. He studied painting at the Istanbul Fine Arts Academy, and then moved to Paris, where from 1959–1964 he attended courses on philosophy and art history. After returning to Turkey, he completed his military service in Hakkari as a reserve officer/teacher. Later, he founded ADA, a publishing company through which he published many major Turkish and world literature books. His novel *O/Hakkari'de bir Mevsim* was made into a film & received awards at the 33rd Berlin Film Festival (1983). He is the recipient of the Sait Faik Award & the Academy of Turkish Language Award.

About the Translator

Fulya PEKER is a New York and Istanbul based theater artist & poet. She holds a BA in Theater (H.U. Ankara State Conservatory), and an MA in Theater, Literature, History, & Criticism (Brooklyn College, CUNY). She has performed in works by Richard Foreman, John Zorn, Robert Ashley, Object Collection, Katsura Kan, and David Michalek. Some of her most prominent NY credits as a writer/director include: *Requiem Æternam Deo*, *The Void*, *The Plague*, and *The Red Book*. She is the founder & artistic director of Katharsis Performance Project & Modern Mythologies Project. Her articles on experimental theater, translations, and poems have been published both in Turkey & in the USA. Currently, she teaches and continues to present workshops & performances internationally.